The spectators qui.... fighters stepped into the square. Taye w... facing a large, heavily muscled black man. Taye was barehanded, but the black man had a knife. Was that allowed? It must be, if the referee didn't take it away or try to stop the fight. Carla couldn't quite suppress her nervous shiver. One of these two men would own her. Taye was almost slender compared to the other man. The smooth way he moved seemed almost balletic to Carla. For all that, the fight was brutal. The black man had pinned Taye Wolfe down with his teeth sunk into his chest, trying to stab him with the knife. But Taye managed to free himself and kick his opponent in the head. He had a gouge in his chest from where the black man had bitten him. Blood ran in a dark stream down his chest. Carla turned her face away, teeth clenched. She didn't look again until she heard Ray shouting that Taye Wolfe had won her. An unearthly howl rose above the roar of the spectators. When she forced herself to look she saw the black man lying still in a pool of blood and Taye with his head flung back and his mouth open in the howl that made her shudder. His mouth closed in a hard grin and his eyes slanted up to meet hers.

Taye Wolfe was her new owner, and he looked as feral as his name.

SLEEPING
WITH THE WOLF

MADDY BARONE

Published 2011
ISBN-13: 978-1466202818
ISBN-10: 1466202815

Manufactured in the United States of America

Cover Art: Lyn Taylor
Book Design: April Martinez

DEDICATION

I dedicate this book to my girlfriends Carla and Lisa for waiting so (im)patiently for each new chapter that I emailed to them. Thank you, ladies, for your encouragement. Without you this book would never have been submitted, much less published. I'll always appreciate what you've done for me. Hugs!

And to Gayle Bitker and Megan Townsend Ramsett, my wonderful beta readers who gave me such good advice. Thank you!

CHAPTER ONE

It wasn't the crowd that made Carla's palms sweat, or even the fact that this crowd was made up exclusively of men who were staring at her. She had spent most of the last five years standing on stage, singing her songs and playing her guitar for thousands of enthusiastic fans at a time, both men and women. She'd even received half a dozen marriage proposals from men she had never met. None of that had ever made her suffer from nerves before. There were only a few hundred men fixated on her here, but her sweaty hands were shaking worse than they ever had before a show. The difference was none of her adoring fans had a snowball's chance in hell of marrying her, but one of these half-savage men lining up to fight for her would be her husband in a few hours. God help them.

How could she have gone from being a rising country music star in the year 2014 to a piece of merchandise in 2064? Useless questions raced angrily around her head, bringing her perilously close to tears, so she scowled at her surroundings.

The theater she was in now must have been a showpiece in its glory days, and maybe a historical site later. Right now it was a shell. The majority of one wall had been knocked out and replaced by mismatched windows so light could come in. The afternoon sun lit the interior like a spotlight on a once elegant but now aging diva. Half the fancy chandeliers were missing, and half of those remaining were missing most of their crystals. The balconies, like the one she stood in now, lined the only intact wall. Carla could see traces of the gold paint that once embellished the ornate carved wood. The raised stage was below and to the left of her balcony, framed in carved wood, but the curtain was gone. The slightly sloping floor was bare wood, marked with rough spots where the seats had once been fastened. The stage had a large square marked off to designate where the fights would take place.

Several of the men made a point of standing below her balcony while they stripped off their shirts and shoes to get ready to fight. They preened for her, stretching muscled lean bodies trying to catch her eye. Some made kissing faces at her. She pointedly ignored them.

Her fingernails, showing only chipped remnants of Cherry Bomb nail lacquer, were ragged while they bit into her palms. If she counted correctly, today was The Day. If her world hadn't ended four days ago she would be singing the national anthem at game five of the World Series tonight. But that world was gone. No cell phones, no cars, no computers, no planes. At least none that could fly … When she left Minneapolis after a show four days ago and boarded a plane to Denver, the world had been sane. Highways were full of cars driven by people who listened to CDs and played DVDs for their children. There were restaurants and grocery stores and malls in every town they flew over. The plane had been full of businessmen tapping away on their laptops and families with teenagers who were glued to their cell phones. And then … the world ended. Somehow the plane had gone fifty years into the future. And this future was after the apocalypse.

Carla glanced over at the woman on the balcony beside hers. Lisa Anton was beautiful. Of course she was beautiful: she was a model. She had long blond hair—natural blond!—perfect skin, perfect body, perfect makeup. At least, her makeup had been perfect when she'd got on the plane. Carla, already in her seat, had cynically tagged her as a Blonde, not too bright, way too vain, and useless. But when the plane went down and the survivors tried to dig through the wreckage to find others, the blonde model had done more than her share of digging and lifting. Her perfect makeup had been smeared all over her face, her perfect clothes torn and dirty. She'd held a little boy while he died and smiled for him the whole time, not crying until after he was gone. While others were hysterical when their cell phones and laptops didn't work she managed to stay calm. When the only surviving member of the plane crew asked for volunteers to walk to try to find help, she immediately offered to go. Three groups of two survivors each set out in different directions to find help. Carla had been impressed by the blonde and hadn't minded being paired up with her as one of the teams going to find help.

Help? A fat lot of help they had gotten. They had been glad and relieved to see the farm people after hiking for a day with no signs of life. The two-lane asphalt road they found was badly cracked and overgrown with grass and weeds. They didn't know where they were, except somewhere between Minneapolis and Denver, without any cell-phone reception. There had been nothing to see but grassy plains for miles. The first town they came to after walking for two hours was totally empty except for rusted shells of cars and sagging buildings. They continued to struggle on, confused by the emptiness around them and worried about the people they left behind. They passed a number of empty ruined farmhouses without ever seeing a person. It made no sense why miles of farm and grazing land were empty. Carla grew up on a ranch in eastern Wyoming, and it wasn't unusual for ranches to be spread far apart, or to see an occasional older house or barn abandoned. But a dozen empty houses? Carla knew there was something weird about that. But she never in a million years would have guessed they had gone fifty years into the future. The crash had been completely unexpected. It was a beautiful day for travel, so when the turbulence hit it caught all the passengers by surprise, and Carla had felt terror close her throat when the plane jolted violently and began to descend. So many had been killed or hurt she felt almost guilty to be merely bruised. But the crash didn't explain the eerie emptiness of these houses and towns.

The walled farming community they found the following morning was weird too. The men guarding the gate had worn plain dark clothes, and held some sort of shotgun or rifle which Carla didn't recognize.

A militant Amish community? Or some strange group like at Waco? If she and Lisa hadn't been so tired and hungry, and if their feet hadn't hurt so much from walking in high-heeled boots, they would have passed on. But these were the first people they had seen, and the people from the plane needed help.

There were plenty of suspicious men, but very few women in the Odessa farming settlement. The farmers wore plain pants and shirts, and their wives wore ankle-length dresses. These farmers did without phones or televisions or computers. They seemed odd but not aggressive in spite of the armed guards at the gate. Their religion was rigid, and all-prevalent. At the midday meal the elder had prayed for "the two worldly strangers from the Times Before whom God sent to us as a gift to save us from the harsh winter." Carla had to bite her tongue to keep from saying something rude. The women had fussed over their blisters and torn clothes and set up skimpy baths of water heated over the stove, like in *Little House on the Prairie*. The men agreed to take Carla and Lisa to the nearest town so they could get help for the survivors.

Right. Fooled by a bunch of Amish farmers. The farmers had taken them in a horse-drawn wagon into a nearby town that looked like a cross between an Old West town and a military base, to the so-called mayor,

Ray Madison. The town was strange, with tall walls made of stone sectioning off some blocks and no signs of technology anywhere. There were no cars, no lights, no fast food places. They passed a building that had once been a popular chain restaurant, but the familiar sign was bleached by age and weather. Some men and boys were on the streets, staring at the two of them like they had two heads each, but they saw no women. Ray had looked them over like they were prime livestock while they had explained about the plane and the survivors needing medical help. Ray hadn't shown much interest in that. He only gave the farmers some boxes and bundles in trade for the two of them. The farmers had left them with Ray. Lisa had cried. Carla had argued. But Ray had rubbed his hands together gleefully and announced that he would offer them as prizes in a Bride Fight. It seemed that two unknown women in their twenties were hot commodities in this future hell.

So that's what they were now, prizes the best fighters could take home. And no help yet for the plane crash survivors. Had either of the other volunteer teams found help? Carla met Lisa's eyes just for a minute and saw the model shaking. Her fair skin showed the signs of tears. Carla hoped her own tanned face was calm. She was so furious she'd like to punch these men. If there hadn't been four guards standing behind her chair she'd have tried to escape. But where could she go?

Ray, the man who had bought her, stepped into her balcony. He smiled at her, showing a few gaps between yellowed teeth. Dental care must be hard to come by in this place. He indicated the men below. "One of those fine men will be yours in just a little while. You got a preference, little lady?"

His father-of-the-bride attitude rubbed Carla the wrong way. "My preference is to go home," she said between clenched teeth.

Ray looked pitying. "Can't," he said patiently. "We've told you over and over that your world doesn't exist anymore. Hasn't for fifty years. Same thing happened a few years back. My missus told you about them other women from the Times Before who showed up out west of here. They never got back neither. They got good husbands now, and couple kids too, I heard. But I ain't never heard nothin' about them complainin'. So, buck up. You got twelve men fighting for you." He sounded like he was congratulating her. "No more than what might be expected, a healthy-looking gal like you. You have a bit of meat on your bones. Gives a man something to hold on to."

Carla's teeth were in danger of shattering. She wore a size twelve, and a size twelve was *not* fat.

"But," Ray went on, "even that skinny yellow-haired gal has eight men fighting for her, including my son."

Ray was proud of his son, and with good reason, Carla had to admit. Eddie was a golden god, as handsome as any model Lisa might have worked with in the past. And he had been nice to her and Lisa when he tried to explain about terrorist nuclear weapons destroying most major US cities fifty years ago, and the asteroid that had hit Texas the following year, and the epidemics that wiped out more women than men, and how hardly anyone alive now even remembered computers or phones. Only a tiny percentage of the population was older than fifty. Eddie had made it plain that this wasn't a dream, and even if they found help for the plane crash survivors they could never go back to their own time. His mother, Darlene, and his sister, Bree, had told them this wasn't the year 2014 anymore, and having two more women in town increased their number to an even two hundred. There were over 4,000 men in the area, and about 1,000 of them were of marriageable age but unmarried. Lots of men would like to marry them, but only a couple dozen would be allowed to enter the Bride Fights. Carla wanted to believe everyone lied to them and it was not 2064. But what else could explain the lack of cars, the lack of modern appliances? Sure, crazy fundamentalist technophobes could all move out to the middle of Nebraska and make their own community without street lights or phones or electricity, but that didn't explain the obvious age of the tumbled buildings or the fact that her cell phone wouldn't place a call to her mother or even 911.

"But you got good men fighting for you," Ray went blithely on. "Like Doug Gray, there. He don't have much to offer a wife, but he's got education. They say he might be able to get some of these gadgets from the Times Before to work someday. You'd like that, hey? And he comes from a pretty well-respected family, too. Bill Russell is a blacksmith. Don't let his size scare you. My wife says he's a real gentleman. He's got a good business. His wife would be taken care of real good. Or there's Taye Wolfe. He's head of the Pack from north of town, and he's got ties to the Lakota hereabouts. Nobody would be stupid enough to mess with his wife. Got probably fifty men under him. They're a bit odd, those wolves, but good people. My daughter says he's a handsome man. Whatchu think?"

Without meaning to, Carla followed Ray's pointing finger. Taye Wolfe was tall and dark, and he had just taken off his shirt, showing an impressive expanse of taut brown skin. Native American? He met her gaze

16

and inclined his head to her before turning away to talk to someone. Carla frowned angrily and jerked her eyes back to Ray.

"You don't have the right to do this," she snapped at Ray. "I am not a slave! You can't sell me off—"

Ray had heard it a dozen times already. "Yes, I can. Common sense says you need to be married. This ain't the Times Before. You are a grown woman without a husband, a father, or a brother. There's too many men here and hardly any women. If you don't get a husband quick the men will fight over you, and not the nice organized fights like these are gonna be. They'll ambush each other, kill each other. They'll commit outright murder. Just to get hold of you. You want that?"

Carla opened her mouth to reply, but he didn't give her a chance.

"And I ain't selling you! All these boys have paid an entrance fee to be able to participate in the Bride Fight. I'll take my fair cut, but the rest goes to the town, to fix the streets and what not. I'm letting only the best men enter. The ones that have enough goods to support a wife, and ones who have a respected position in the town. Sure, Doug Gray's not as well off as the rest of these others, but he's respected. All of 'em are good fighters. The best fighter deserves to have a wife. That way the best genes will pass on to the next generation."

17

Carla said a word she seldom used.

"And," Ray went on, raising his voice to cover her profanity, "my wife got final pick of who got to enter. She made sure all of the fighters are good men. They'll treat you right. She thinks any of these men would be good enough for our own daughter. If they're good enough for Bree, they're good enough for you." He gave her a fierce nod. "Now I'm going to go over to the other gal and give her a pep talk too."

Carla forced her fists open and took deep breaths, not bothering to watch Ray leave. Pep talk. Right.

"Ma'am?"

A low, deep voice made her jump. It was Taye Wolfe, standing just below the balcony. Carla realized that he *was* a handsome man, with thick shiny black hair cut neatly at his nape, but long enough to fall into his eyes. His eyes were dark too, with surprisingly long lashes, under elegantly curved black brows. And he was younger than she had thought, maybe only twenty-three or twenty-four. His mouth was full and soft, a contrast to the hard angle of his jaw, and a hint of a dimple showed at the corner of his mouth.

"Ma'am," he said again. "I heard that you are from the Times Before, and you don't want to be here. Is that so?"

Maybe it was her love of putting sounds together

to create music that made his deep voice so attractive to her. It gave her shivers. She leaned over the balcony, holding her long walnut brown hair back so it wouldn't fall past the railing. "Yes! I need to go back to the plane! People are dying!" She looked around and noticed several of the other fighters scowling at Taye. She lowered her voice. "Can you help me get away?"

"No, ma'am." His teeth were very white against his brown face when he smiled at her. "I plan to win this fight and marry you. But I want you to know that I'll always take good care of you. I don't know you yet, but I hope we'll love each other someday. Until then I can promise you respect and gentleness." He nodded once and walked away, leaving her gaping after him. He paused and turned back. "And I think I should tell you that I've read a bunch of those romance novels from the Times Before, and I know what a woman likes. I promise you'll be satisfied in our bed." He smiled again, a wicked white slash in his brown face, and sauntered away. Carla stared after him, appreciating the narrow waist and wide shoulders before remembering why he was here. Curse him. Curse them all!

Carla's thoughts raced around her head. Like it or not, she was going home with a stranger after this tournament. Did she have anything in her purse that could be used as a weapon? She had a lot to choose from in there. After carrying it for a day and a half she knew how much it weighed. She picked it up from the floor beside her and rummaged through it, cataloging its contents. She was vaguely aware that Ray was down on the stage now, making announcements. She heard her name and the roar of applause from the crowd and looked out at them, glaring. Now, what did she have? Keys for an apartment and car that had no doubt been destroyed in the past fifty years. Wallet with useless money and credit cards. Knitting needle? That could be a weapon, but she was knitting socks on tiny double-pointed needles that her brother called toothpicks, so probably not. Nail file? It was blunt and pretty small, from a purse-size travel kit. Darn the airline security regulations. She was wearing a leather belt with her barrel-racing championship buckle. The buckle was large and solid. If she swung it by the belt and hit someone, it could cause a lot of damage. Even kill a person. But was she capable of that?

The preliminary fights had already taken place when she decided to start paying attention. By the time she figured out what was going on, there were only eight men left on the stage aside from the referees, four fighting for her and four for Lisa. The contenders for her were on the right. She knew this because Taye Wolfe and Doug Gray were there. Lisa's men, including

Eddie, were on the left. Eddie kissed his fingertips and flicked his hand up, smiling at Lisa in the balcony besides hers.

Carla looked over at Lisa. The blonde tried to smile at Eddie, but she was terrified, and not hiding it well. Eddie would probably make an okay husband. Carla hoped he would win. He would treat Lisa nicely. Only two days ago Lisa had been only a name and a picture in magazine. Now she was like a sister. Carla wanted Lisa to be okay and happy, if possible. She looked down at the stage again, and her eyes met Taye Wolfe's. His face was tilted down so that when he looked up at her it was from under level brows. His dimple flashed with his quick smile. Carla folded her arms and glared briefly before looking away.

She couldn't help but look, though, when Taye and Doug Gray went into the square and both turned to face her. They nodded formally, almost like a bow, then shook hands, and at a word from one of the referees began to fight. It was a brutal mixture of boxing and wrestling. With four brothers, Carla had seen plenty of fights, but this was vicious. Compared to Taye Wolfe, Doug Gray was lanky, not as muscular. He fought well, though. Taye was hurt, but he won in the end, pinning his opponent in a strangle hold. Doug Gray slapped his hand against the floor to signal his defeat. Taye

Wolfe helped him up and they shook hands. Doug Gray nodded to Carla, and Taye Wolfe sent her another wicked smile. Jerk. Did he think she was glad he had won? She looked away and yawned as if bored.

But actually, her stomach was jumping around so much she thought she might throw up. She barely watched the next fights because she wasn't sure she could keep her face cool. She knew Eddie won his last fight because Lisa gave a half sob and said, "Thank God!" audibly, and then the spectators began applauding and chanting Eddie's name. That was good. Lisa liked Eddie, and Eddie was obviously smitten with her. Ray's voice was proud when he announced that the hand of Miss Lisa Anton had been won by Eddie Madison.

The spectators quieted down when the last two fighters stepped into the square. Taye Wolfe was facing a large, heavily muscled black man. Wasn't he the blacksmith Ray had pointed out to her? Taye was barehanded, but the black man had a knife. Was that allowed? It must be, if the referee didn't take it away or try to stop the fight. Carla couldn't quite suppress her nervous shiver. One of these two men would own her. Taye was almost slender compared to the other man. The smooth way he moved seemed like a ballet to Carla. For all that, the fight was brutal. The black man had pinned Taye Wolfe down with his teeth sunk into his chest, trying to stab him with the knife. But Taye managed to free himself and kick his opponent in the head. He had a gouge in his chest from where the black man had bitten him. Blood ran in a dark stream down his chest. Carla turned her face away, teeth clenched. She didn't look again until she heard Ray shouting that Taye Wolfe had won her. An unearthly howl rose above the roar of the spectators. When she forced herself to look she saw the black man lying still in a pool of blood and Taye with his head flung back and his mouth open in the howl that made her shudder. His teeth closed in a hard grin and his eyes slanted to look up at her with fierce triumph.

Taye Wolfe was her new owner, and he looked as feral as his name.

Chapter Two

The fights had been hard, especially the final bout. Taye knew he was bleeding from the slice across his forearm and the bite over his right pec, but he didn't care. He screamed his victory, his howl rising above the roar of the crowd. The first thing he saw when he finished was Eddie Madison with his arm tenderly around his prize, and the trusting way she laid her cheek against his shoulder. Taye looked up at the balcony where his own prize stood. Surely now she would have lost that aloof expression of disdain. Now she would know he was worthy of her.

But no, Carla had lost the disdain, but replaced it with disgust. Horror? Fear? That wasn't right. His wolf's protective instincts took over. Genetics and adrenaline gave him the strength to leap from the stage to the balcony. Her hair swung when she jerked back from his reaching hands. Her hazel eyes were wide, going from the stage where he had been standing to him now standing in front of her, before fixing on the blood seeping down his chest and then jerking up to his face.

"Don't touch me!" she hissed.

"Shh," he soothed gently. "It's OK."

"Yeah, right," she snapped. "You touch me and you'll be sorry."

She was trying to hide it, but he could smell her fear. It hurt him. He pulled back a little. "Don't be afraid. I promise, all I want is for you to be happy. For us to be happy."

Her sour expression doubted him. "Yeah, right," she said again.

His mate was beautiful even with a sour expression. Her face was triangular with a broad forehead tapering to a narrow, stubborn chin. Greenish eyes were outlined with long dark lashes, and her mouth was made up of a narrow upper lip and a plump lower lip. Her legs were long, too, and he wanted to wrap them around his waist and put her against the wall … No, better to not think of that yet. The urge to touch her, to feel that full red lower lip against his was overpowering, but he forced himself to keep a little space between them. "Don't be afraid," he said again. "I'll be a good husband. I'll take good care of you and our children."

The scent of her fear grew stronger. His words weren't working. She didn't know him yet. Time would show her that she was safe with him. He signaled to Pete and Jay, his packmates standing below the balcony as guards. Here at a public contest like a Bride Fight he should be guaranteed safety, but the three-mile walk home could be an invitation for sore losers to try to steal the prize they had lost. He and his Pack would need to be extra vigilant. "Let's go home, wife."

Carla folded her arms over her chest. "I'm not your wife."

"Yeah, you are."

"Since when?" she challenged. "I don't remember being invited to the ceremony."

Taye caught hold of his patience. "I won the Bride Fight, remember? Didn't you hear Ray make the announcement? You're mine now."

"That's it?" Her voice rose sharply. She clutched her leather satchel against her chest like a shield. "That's the entire ceremony? What about the church? What about the vows?"

Taye stared at her strangely for a moment, trying to

remember anything about the marriage customs from the Times Before. "We don't have a church or a priest here. Don't need 'em to be married. You want vows? I'll make vows to you. I promise to take care of you as long as I live. If there's only enough food for one of us, you'll get it. I'll keep you warm when it's cold. Anyone who tries to hurt you will have to go through me first. How's that?"

"Those aren't wedding vows!"

Taye shrugged. His new mate was obviously too upset to be reasonable. Taye shook his head, picked her up with one arm under her knees and the other around her shoulders and jumped out the balcony. The shriek she let out almost popped his eardrums. She let go of the satchel to clutch at him. He landed and reluctantly set her on the floor. For just a second her arms remained clenched around his neck. But she remembered herself too soon and scrambled out of his arms.

"What the h—How did y—ARE YOU CRAZY?" she screeched. She stumbled in her hurry to back away. "Don't ever do that to me again!"

"All right," he agreed mildly. A quick slash of his hand killed Pete and Jay's grins. Jay held out his shirt and shoes. "I'll get my things on." A smear of his blood stained her green blouse at the shoulder and breast. It made him perversely happy to see that. All the spectators would know she belonged to him. "Why don't you say good-bye to your friend before we leave?"

Lisa Anton was standing in the embrace of Eddie's arms, blue eyes wide, eyelashes dark and spiky with tears. Carla's brown leather satchel hung from her free hand. Unlike Carla, the blonde seemed content to let her husband hold her. She held the leather satchel out. "Carla, here's your purse. Are you … Are you okay?"

"Peachy," Carla snapped. Taye was bent over putting on his shoes, so he couldn't see her face, but he heard her voice soften. "Sorry. Yeah, I'm okay. You?"

Lisa's pale hair rippled when she nodded. "Yeah. But Eddie says he doesn't see much of Taye or his Pack. I'll miss you."

Carla's eyes were gleaming. With tears? "I'll miss you too."

Yes, tears. But she was blinking hard, daring them to fall. Taye straightened and nodded once at Eddie Madison. "You have free passage if you want to bring your wife for a visit. Send a message ahead. I'll clear it for you."

Eddie smiled. Taye had never in his life been attracted to a man, but even he felt the sensual beauty of that smile. "Thanks. Lisa will like that. After the honeymoon we'll take you up on that."

Eddie's mate flushed a delicate pink, and she smiled

at her new husband's mention of a honeymoon. His own mate jerked her chin up and glared at him. Taye hoped that wasn't a bad sign for his own honeymoon. He had been looking forward to tonight for years. The sooner they got home, the sooner he could begin gentling his mate.

"We better get moving. We need to get home before dark. Eddie. Ma'am." He nodded at the blonde politely. "Congratulations."

CHAPTER THREE

It had been warm inside the theater, but out here on the street with the sun going down and the wind cutting through her clothes, Carla shivered. It was the cold that made her shiver, not fear of the savage walking alongside her. Definitely. She paused to dig her jacket out of her overgrown handbag. Taye stopped immediately and looked at her with a small frown, and so did the other two, but with bigger frowns.

"I'm cold," she said curtly, shrugging the jacket on. It was one of her favorites, short-waisted so it wouldn't cover her rodeo belt buckle, made of supple suede dyed burgundy red with fringe dripping off the arms. It had matched her high-heeled pointy-toed cowboy boots, except the cowboy boots were now so scuffed and dirty that they looked piebald brown. Life in the public eye had taught both Lisa and her to carry necessities like basic toiletries, water and snacks, and a change of underwear in their purses, so they had all kinds of helpful essentials. Too bad she hadn't packed a pair of walking shoes in her purse. "If you're cold," Taye suggested, holding out his arms.

He was wearing only a thin cotton shirt that looked like it was a size too small, so each muscle in his upper arms, chest, and belly was obvious. "No, thank you," she snapped, starting forward again. But she peeked at him, looking at the blood staining his shirt on the right side of his chest and the dried blood on his forearm. "Aren't you hur—cold?"

"Nah," he shrugged. His white, white teeth glowed briefly in the dimming light. "Unless you're offering to warm me up?"

Carla stared stonily straight ahead and marched on. The man behind them made a sound like a smothered laugh. Taye just shrugged and walked beside her, moving smoothly and easily in spite of his obvious injuries. Carla refused to feel sorry for him. If he was hurt it was his own fault. No one made him enter that stupid fight. Of course, if he hadn't won it would have been somebody else. She could be going home with someone else. Maybe someone even worse.

For the first twenty minutes she strode sullenly along the broken pavement. The next quarter hour she focused on evil thoughts to help her hide her limp. But Taye, curse him, was too observant, and he picked her up like a baby, carrying her several strides before she demanded furiously to be put down.

"Your feet gotta be hurting you," he returned casually. "I'll carry you the last mile home."

Carla drew in a breath to scream at him, but wrestled the urge down. She was not going to act like some too-stupid-to-live heroine in a cheap romance novel. She stuck her chin in the air and pretended to not notice him. It was hard, though, when he was so warm and smelled so good. How he could smell so good when he was sweaty and bloody she didn't know, but he did. She breathed in his enticing scent for only a couple minutes before he stiffened and lowered her gently to the ground.

"Stay here," he murmured.

"Wha—" she began.

Four men came out of nowhere, armed with clubs and something shiny—knives?—and attacked Taye and his two friends. Carla stared in disbelief as a fifth man came from a different direction right at her. He said something to her. It sounded like something about helping her? But Carla concluded from the bulge in the front of his pants he was too excited about the prospect of helping her to be trusted. When he tried to take her arm she whipped the pointy toe of her cowboy boot into his groin with all the strength she could muster. He screamed like a woman and fell over, curling himself into a fetal position. Carla hopped back from him right into another man. She whirled, poising herself for another kick, but it was Taye, who was staring at the man writhing on the asphalt.

"Ouch," he said, something between respect and glee threading his deep voice.

"Damn, Chief," said one of his friends admiringly. "She's gonna make one hell of a Lupa."

Carla glared, trying to hide her fear and confusion. Taye was smiling at her, a wide grin of approval and appreciation. The man who had spoken was now looking around, back in guard mode. The second of Taye's friends was nowhere to be seen, but a large gray dog was sniffing around the four men bleeding on the ground. Taye nodded to the dog and told it to keep its ears and nose open and give a warning if it found anything, as if it could understand everything he said; then he put his large callused hand over Carla's wrist firmly.

"We have to hurry. Sorry 'bout your feet hurting,

but I gotta keep myself ready to fight. I can't carry you. We need to get you home before any other women stealers come after you. Ready? Run!"

It was the closest to a five-minute mile Carla had ever run, and if Taye hadn't been towing her along by her wrist she would have fallen blocks behind the two men and the gray dog. Her once-fashionable boots were killing her. So were her calves, her ankles, and her thighs. It looked like Taye and his friends lived in a one-story motel surrounded by a high chain-link fence. She thought she recognized a tall sign, almost too faded to be readable, to be the logo for a popular chain motel. After they ran through the fence gate to a grassy area which must have been the parking lot once upon a time, Taye finally let her stop running, so she thought this must be home. She put her hands on her knees and leaned over to gasp air back into her lungs, and swore she would start to exercise more. The tall chain-link fence that went around the property was patrolled by men who stared at her.

So this was home? A dumpy roach motel at the edge of a broken prairie town? At least Ray lived in a large Victorian mansion. Taye had left her side to talk quietly with some of the men. Carla counted four men strolling along the fence like sentries. Taye was smiling broadly at something one of them had said when he turned to look at her. His eyes were almost a physical weight as his smile turned somehow intimate. She admitted privately that he was handsome. Sometimes he looked like he was sixteen years old. His face sometimes seemed soft, almost boyish with full lips, but other times looked hard with a square jaw and high cheekbones and fierce dark eyes. His face might sometimes look boyish, but the broad, muscled chest and chiseled abs were completely grown up. He saw her looking at him. In the dark he couldn't have seen her appreciation for his physique, but she was careful to glance away as if bored.

He walked over to her and swept his arm around her waist, pulling her with him towards the motel. "Come on," he murmured. "Let's get you inside so you can warm up and take off your boots."

She let him pull her along. He smelled so good. Was he wearing some really subtle cologne? She bent her face a quarter inch towards his shoulder and sniffed discreetly. Maybe it was just him.

Of course, he noticed. His mouth quirked in a half smile. "Like my scent?" he teased. "*You* smell delicious, sweetheart. It's the mating scent. Mates always smell alluring to each other."

Carla gritted her teeth and ignored him, his sexy voice, and his yummy scent. They entered what had once been the motel lobby. She didn't know how it had been decorated back in the first decade of the 21st century, but now it looked like an Old West-themed lounge. There were a bunch of wooden chairs draped with furs around square wood tables which held oil lamps and decks of cards, sawhorses with blankets draped over them, and a large stone fireplace. The floors were bare wood, but not rough wood like in the theater. It was smooth and had been coated with something to make it shiny. It actually looked pretty nice.

"I'll give you a full tour later," Taye said in her ear. "This is the rec room. The boys hang out here most of the time. That room over there on the left is the dining hall. And through here are the rooms we live in. Most of the men have a room to themselves. I have a set of rooms. They connect. So we'll have a room for sleeping and a room for you to do your sewing or whatever you like in. It'll be private, just for you."

Carla hoped it had a bed or a couch for her to sleep on, because she wasn't sleeping in his room.

"In back we have a stable and a garden," he continued.

Carla stopped thinking about the sleeping arrangements. "You have horses? You ride?"

Taye shook his head. "Mostly pack horses, to carry trade goods. For traveling, we mostly run when we want to go somewhere. Our kin keep their horses there when they come to town to visit. You ride?"

"I grew up on a ranch," Carla said. She patted her belt buckle. "I barrel raced all during high school and for a few years afterwards."

Taye nodded dubiously. He wasn't sure what the draw of racing a barrel would be, but his mate seemed pretty proud of it. "I'll get you a horse."

"I have a h…" Carla trailed off. Her horse was at her parents' place, fifty years in the past. It hurt to think about it, so she didn't. The hall he was leading her down was narrow and dim. She noticed the walls were bare. Any boring motel art had been removed along with the light fixtures. The doors still looked solid, with their brass numbers still attached.

Taye stopped in front room 121 and opened the door. "This is our room. I guess, uh, it's pretty plain. But you can decorate some if you want."

Actually, Carla admitted, it was nice. Homey. The bed was a double, the frame bolted to the floor just as it had been fifty years ago. It was covered by a patchwork quilt made of denim squares. Hopefully the mattress was not fifty years old. Not that it mattered since she wasn't going to be sleeping on it. Curtains made of rough woven denim were pulled back so the setting sun could come in through the long windows. In one corner was a small round table with two straight-backed chairs. The polished wood floor was covered by two good-sized oval rag rugs, one beside the bed and the other in front of a sofa made from carved wood slats and cushions made of the same denim squares. The original dresser was against the wall, the mirror a little wavy.

Taye ushered her over to the couch and told her to sit, then closed the curtains and went around and lit a few lamps. Carla ignored his order to sit, dumped her purse on the floor by the couch and limped to the adjoining room. It was completely empty, not a stick of furniture in it. She went back to the couch. It was comfortable enough. She was so tired she would sleep fine right where she was. She noticed a tattered paperback book on the end table, its cover curled up and almost bleached of color. She tried to read the title, expecting a western or a thriller. *Love's Last Passion*? *Love's Lost Passion*? Good grief. How had that survived the apocalypse? She remembered Taye mentioning something about reading romance novels. *So he could please her in bed?* Yikes!

"We'll get you what you need for your private room." Taye knelt before her and grabbed one of her boots. "Wiggle your foot, sweetheart. Let's get these off."

Carla straightened with a snap. "I can do it. You should clean up your cuts. You know, from the fight."

"Don't worry about them. They're fine."

Carla snatched her foot away from him. "I can do it! And there's a lot of blood on your shirt. You should take care of that. It could get infected."

Taye was shaking his head at her. "The Pack don't get infections. But I'll clean up if it will make you happy. Then I'll go get us some food. Stay in here, okay? The boys are pretty curious about you. I don't want you to run into any of them yet without me along."

Alone in the room, Carla removed her jacket and took off her boots. She considered leaving the boots on since they were the only weapons she had, but she had seen Taye fight. She was pretty sure she was defenseless against him. Besides, her feet hurt bad. She held her feet up one at a time to the lamplight and saw oozing blisters. She should clean them. She wondered what the bathroom was like, and wandered over to the door she hadn't gone through yet. The bathroom looked exactly like a bathroom from home, absolutely pristine, with a bucket full of water on the floor beside the tub. What she wouldn't give for a hot bath. Or a flushing toilet. Or any running water. Hotel towels must be indestructible. Two hung over the rail above the toilet, a bit gray but clean. She dipped a corner of one in the bucket of water and used it to clean her feet as well as she could.

Taye returned in fifteen minutes. He was wearing only cut-off shorts and carried a tray. He set the tray down on the round table in the corner and turned to face her. She examined his chest only because she wanted to see how bad the cut was. Yep, that was the only reason. Of course, she had to admit it was a very nice chest. The man was buff. But she couldn't see any cut, at least not that would have bled so much. Maybe it had been someone else's blood? The slice on the inside of his forearm was only a thin red line against his brown skin. She was sure he had been badly hurt. She had a blood smear on her shirt from when he had grabbed her and jumped over the edge of the balcony to the floor. How had he done that? He was strong, yes, but no one was that strong. She was so lost in thought that he was standing right in front of her before she saw him move.

"Come on, let's eat."

If Carla hadn't been so hungry she would have resisted. But she was starving. Breakfast had been a long time ago. She sat at the table and let him serve her. But when Carla saw the blood oozing out of the meat she almost gagged. "Didn't you cook it?" she demanded.

"Sure. See? It's brown on the outside."

"It's red on the inside!"

Taye put his knife down and looked at her with a small frown. "You like your meat brown all the way through?" He sounded horrified.

"Yes, I like it cooked. Sheesh."

"None of us eat our meat all brown. And when we're in our fur we don't always cook it at all. You can make yours the way you like it from now on. Just remember to leave ours nice and red. For tonight, you can eat it like this or fill up on potatoes and greens."

Carla sawed off all the mostly done edges of her steak, and Taye gave her his too, and she ate those and the potatoes and mushy green beans. All in all it wasn't too bad. And the bread was really good. "So, who does the cooking around here?"

Taye slathered more butter on his bread. "The boys take turns. Now that you're here, you can take over."

Carla played with the last few beans on her plate. "How many live here?"

"Forty-eight. Forty-nine, including you. There's another hundred fifty or so who aren't Pack. They don't live in the den here, but we watch over them."

"How many women?"

"One."

"Two, including me?"

"Nah, that is including you."

41

Carla put her silverware down carefully, not wanting to be holding a knife if she lost her temper. "I am the only woman here? Just me?"

"Yeah. You are the only female member of the Pack. The Lupa, the Alpha Female."

"And you think I'm going to cook and clean for all of you?"

Taye looked surprised by the way her voice escalated. "You're a woman," he pointed out reasonably, as if she had somehow forgotten that.

"So? Big deal! Let me tell you something. Where I come from women aren't slaves. We don't automatically do all the cooking and cleaning just because we're female. So get this: *I am not your maid!*"

"You're my mate, not maid."

Carla glared. "Because you 'won' me in some stupid testosterone contest," she sneered.

Taye leaned across the table and picked up her clenched fists in his warm callused hands. That luscious scent poured over her. "Sweetheart, you aren't my mate because I won the Bride Fight. I won the Bride Fight because you're my mate. Last night when I saw you at Ray's I knew you were my mate. I wouldn't have entered if you weren't."

"You *saw* me? When did you see me?"

"At Ray's, last night. A little after dark. He sent

42

out the notice for the Bride Fight that afternoon. Just about every man in the Pack went to Ray's to see if you might be the one his wolf chose to be his mate. You were in a room, combing your hair in a mirror. Only it wasn't a mirror. It was one of those windows where people can see in but not out." Taye's voice sank to a growling whisper. "I knew you were my mate when I saw you. All those men, staring at you, imagining you in their beds ... I let them live. Even today, when I was fighting, I let them live. But it was hard." His eyes seemed to almost glow in the lamp light." Those fools who tried to take you away from me on the way home tonight ... They deserved to die for even thinking of touching you. The one who tried to grab you—" His face contorted for a moment, turning so savage that she froze. "If you hadn't already dealt with him yourself I would've torn his throat out."

His hands were so warm and he smelled so good that Carla had to try to twist her hands away so she wouldn't do something that would encourage him. He was appealing but terrifying. He talked about killing men like she talked about swatting flies. But he wouldn't let go of her hands.

"You're afraid of me!" he accused. "Don't be. I would never hurt you. You're mine." He pulled her hands to his face and inhaled deeply.

"Stop that!" she said sharply. "I'm not afraid of you." This was crazy. She was trapped here, like she was some sort of a mail-order bride from the 1800s, expected to cook and clean for a pack of half-wild bachelors, and do more for him at night. She glanced quickly at the bed, and away again. A few days ago she had been a successful music artist from the 21st century, starting to make it big with the second single from her debut CD just breaking into the Top Ten. What was she now? A glorified whore? Hot tears burned her eyes but she refused to cry. She finally managed to jerk her hands away to swipe one under her nose. "Look, we need to get some things straight, okay? I am not going to sleep with you. I don't even know you."

Taye frowned, his golden face sad but not angry. "I can understand how you feel. But it's half killing me to stay this far away from you." At her furious glare, which she used to cover her fear, he sighed. "You're right. We need to talk."

He leaned back in his chair and crossed his arms over his beautiful, bare chest. Carla made herself look away from the inviting golden skin. He was so tempting. In some ways it would be so easy to let him take her to bed. But she had slept with only two men in her life, both of whom she'd been in love with and planning a future with. Derek McDonald had been her high school sweetheart, but when he went to college they had drifted apart. Really, they'd probably been too young to even think of getting married. And Josh Oldham ... Even now she inwardly flinched at his memory. He had dumped her for a model a year and a half ago. When she had won the Country Music Star competition last year he had sent her a dozen roses and a card with a sucking-up message about them getting together for dinner sometime. Yeah, right. She had thrown the card away and donated the roses to a hospital.

"Sweetheart, what makes you look like that?"

Carla narrowed her eyes further, enough to start a headache, and decided to be perfectly honest. Maybe that would scare him off. "I don't like men. I don't trust men. I had one a couple years ago. He left me because he found another woman he liked better. Really ruined the whole I-love-you-until-death-do-us-part thing. So don't expect me to fall head over heels in love with you."

Taye's arms fell limply and his jaw dropped. "A man *left* you? He had you and he left you?" He rubbed his eyes tiredly. "I've heard there were plenty of women in the Times Before, but what kind of man would leave his woman? I won't ever do that to you. We're mates, and wolves mate for life."

"Uh-huh." Carla eyed him doubtfully. "So what's

my name supposed to be now? Carla Wolfe?"

"That's what the people in town will call you. But we'll call you Lupa." Taye stood and began piling their empty plates on the tray. He carried it over to the door and put it in the hall outside. He closed the door and leaned on it, staring at her with his dark eyes shimmering like a cat's in the dim lamp light. "I need to tell you some things. You're from the Times Before, so you won't know about us. It will sound crazy, but I'm telling the truth. I'm a wolf. I'm the Alpha wolf of this Pack, and of the forty-eight boys in the pack, thirty-two others are wolves too."

"Uh, okay. They're your brothers and cousins? Taye Wolfe and his Wolfe Pack. Ha-ha. Cute. Sounds like a band from the '60s."

"Brothers in fur, and most of them are cousins by blood. Wolf-born we call it. Carla—" It was the first time he had used her name, and it jolted her as much as his serious tone. "—I don't want any secrets between us, ever. I don't want us to be fighting because we don't take the time to talk about things. I'm a wolf. And I'm not talking about my family name. Most of the time I'm a man, but sometimes I'm a wolf." He searched her face anxiously, then sighed sadly. "You don't understand a word I'm trying to tell you."

Carla carefully brushed some bread crumbs off the

arm of the chair, avoiding looking at him because she was wondering if he were a little touched. "Actually, no."

"I guess I'll have to show you. Remember, I'm your mate. I'll never hurt you."

He raised his arms and took a step forward. Carla frowned and blinked. His arms slimmed, turned hairy gray and hit the floor, his nails tapping against the bare wood. What? Where did—? Carla leapt out of the chair, gaping at the big gray dog standing by the door. No, not a dog. A wolf! Taye was a werewolf! She scrambled back, slamming painfully into the wall. The big wolf—he must outweigh her by a couple hundred pounds!—walked slowly toward her, one large paw at a time. He nudged his nose under her hand and flipped it over his head, just like the farm dog back home, wanting his ears scratched. Her legs gave out and she slid against the wall to the floor. The wolf laid his muzzle on her shoulder, nuzzling her neck through her hair. Her terror subsided slightly when she caught his scent. It really was Taye. He'd kept talking about the Pack, and mates, and … Oh, God. This is what Ray had meant when he called Taye's Pack 'those wolves.'

"Oh, my God," she whispered. "It's you. You're…" Her hand shook when she reached to pet the huge head lying heavy on her shoulder. The warmth of his thick gray fur bled into her when he leaned his body against her. "You're a werewolf."

A wave of hot air blew against her, and somehow she found herself petting short black hair, pressed against warm bare brown skin. She froze, jerking her hand away. Taye had his face pressed against her neck, breathing deeply. "A wolf," he murmured into her hair. "Not a werewolf. That's only in books. I am not controlled by the moon, and I sure don't eat humans." He sniffed delicately under her ear and kissed the edge of her jaw. "Well, I might eat you, but only in the good way." His hand drifted toward her breast.

Carla gave him a shove that made absolutely no impact on him. "Stop that!" she screeched wildly. "Let me go! I already said I wasn't going to sleep with you. If you try to force me I'll fight."

He lifted his head sharply. "Force—"

She cut him off, voice still high and wild. "I won't win, I know I won't win, but I won't make it easy for you! I swear—"

Taye stood up, taking her with him with no effort and standing her on her feet before stepping away. His face was angry—and hurt?—when he scowled at her. "I'm not a rapist," he snarled. "I won't force you." He swung away, raking a hand through his hair. "Why would you think I would hurt you like that?" he demanded, turning back to her. "What have I done to make you believe I would hurt you?"

Carla opened her mouth to snap out examples, and after a few moments of reviewing his actions throughout the day, closed it. "Nothing," she admitted reluctantly. She dug a bare toe into the smooth wood of the floor. "I just don't ... It's just that everything has gone crazy. I don't know where I am, or how I got here or ... or anything. I don't know *you*! And now I'm supposed to be married to you? Mated to you? Whatever that is, *and* chief cook and bottle washer to a bunch of we—wolves! I don't know what's going on. I don't know how I can live here, in this crazy time. I don't know anything except *I want to go home!*"

———

Taye flinched at her wail. The wolf inside him was frantic to comfort his mate. Her tears were killing him. He lost his own anger and pulled her reluctant body against his chest. "Shh," he soothed. "It's going to be okay. We'll work it out." Without her boots the top of her head was only a little above his shoulder, putting her eyes right at his collarbone. All at once her spine melted and she slumped against him, weeping. Holding her like this, rubbing a hand over her cold arms, feeling her tears on his shoulder, was amazing.

She was actually clutching his arms. Her trust calmed his wolf. He picked her up and carried her to the bed, setting her on the edge. She made to push away, but he knelt on the floor and let her put a little distance between them, still smoothing his hands over her arms. "Until you feel different, this bed is only for sleeping, okay? Don't be afraid that I will ambush you during the night. I can wait until you're ready."

"I can sleep on the couch," she offered hopefully.

The wolf that lived inside him, the one who had chosen her for his mate, didn't like that idea. He was Alpha; no one ever went against his wishes. He shook his head. "No, we'll share the bed."

"It's not that big," she argued, "and you are."

"We'll share the bed," he said with finality. He watched her acceptance but her scent indicated she was still frightened. Maybe she needed some time to herself. Heaven knew he did. His wolf wanted his mate and didn't understand why Taye wasn't making love to her right now. "I'm going out for a run. I'll be gone about two hours." He waved at the bathroom. "You want a bath while I'm out?"

He saw she perked up a little. "A bath? A real bath?"

He led her to the bathroom. Leaning over the tub he put the drain stopper down and turned the water on. "There's soap there, and towels."

Her eyes were fixed with something close to lust on the steam rising from the water pouring from the faucet. "You have running water? Hot running water?"

Apparently he had finally done something right. "Yeah. The boys have kept this water warm ever since we got home. I figured you'd like to take a hot bath after we … Um. I've heard that women are a bit sore after the first time or two they make love."

The blissful look on Carla's face altered to surprise. "I'm not a virgin."

Rage punched him in the gut, taking his breath away. She had said she had had a man. She had said that. But he'd thought they had only been courting. He simply couldn't imagine any man leaving the woman who gave him her body. Making love was binding. What lousy cur would abandon his wife for another woman? He deserved to have his throat ripped out and his entrails burned.

"You said no secrets," Carla reminded him anxiously.

The sharp scent of her fear helped him force back the rage. "I'm not angry. Not at you," he clarified. "That—" He resorted to Lakota because he couldn't think of the right words in English to describe the evil man who had abandoned her. "You just relax and enjoy your bath." He patted her shoulder. "I'll be back in a couple hours." He couldn't resist a quick sniff of her neck, a brushed kiss over her jaw.

He took the memory of her scent with him on his run. Her scent mingled with the memories of his parents and rocky beginnings of their relationship. At the edge of the den he gestured Sky and Quill over and invited them to go hunting with him. If they wondered what a newly mated wolf was doing away from his mate on their first night together they didn't say anything. They had come from the Clan that lived on the plains a few months ago to live near a town and learn how to interact with settled humans. Neither of them had earned the right to question him, which was why he had chosen them and not wolves from his Pack. Part of him wanted to be alone, but he knew he was too frazzled to watch his back properly. The two younger wolves would be able to watch out for him. They changed and took off for the open land outside of town. He needed to kill something, and since his mate's former man was out of his reach he'd settle for a deer or three.

It was past midnight before they returned to the den. He paused in the kitchen to wash the blood from his body and hair and pull on a pair of sweatpants. He didn't want to alarm his mate by sleeping naked as he usually did. She was sleeping soundly, curled on her side facing the door, but he was careful to be silent when he got into bed behind her. Even with the blankets the flesh of her arms was cold. She was wearing one of his short-sleeved shirts, and her jeans. Most humans were cold compared to wolves, but she was colder than most. He wrapped his warmth around her, his bare chest to her back, his knees behind hers, his arm draped over her waist. She slept through it, only murmuring something about warm, and wiggling her bottom snugly into his groin. Taye clenched his teeth, wondering if she should sleep on the couch after all. This was going to be torture. But she sighed in her sleep and laid her arm over his where it curled over her waist in a gesture so trusting it soothed him. Maybe it would be worth it. He inhaled her delicious scent and kissed her nape through her hair. He would spend time with her so she could get to know him. They would talk together. He would heat water so she'd get a hot bath everyday if that's what it took to win her. Soon they would be doing more than just sleeping in this bed.

Chapter Four

Taye woke late, feeling almost peaceful. He inhaled the wonderful scent of his mate lingering in the bedclothes but knew immediately she was not beside him. He heard the shower running and realized he had been woken by a soft yelp from the bathroom. He relaxed against the pillow that smelled of Carla and listened to her moving around the bathroom. After a few minutes she came out, dressed except for her socks and boots, her wet hair wrapped in a towel. She rubbed her arms briskly. He kept his eyes mostly closed so he could watch her unobserved as she went to the bureau mirror to comb out her hair. When he heard her teeth chatter he stopped pretending. Wolves didn't feel the cold like humans did, so fifty degrees was comfortable for him. For her, though, he would need to have a fire to keep her warm. He would see to that today.

He came out of bed with a smooth, stretching yawn. "Good morning. Did you sleep well?" He ran a gentle finger over her cold cheek. "You're awfully cold. Will you let me hold you? I can warm you up."

She jerked away. "No, thank you," she said with frigid courtesy.

His wolf howled silently at him to take care of his mate. He wrestled with his Alpha instinct to command and won. "You're cold," he pointed out in his most reasonable voice. "I'm a wolf. I'm always hot. I can get you hot too."

She looked at him sharply, probably looking for innuendo, but he had been sincere. She seemed to realize it, because she stepped close to him and shook. "I didn't think the shower would be cold," she shuddered.

"Water has to be heated. Your hair is wet," he chided. He reached for the dropped towel and wrapped her hair up again. "It's too cold for a human woman to walk around with wet hair."

"I know, I forgot about the blow drier not working."

Taye let her go for a moment to pull an extra blanket out of a drawer. He draped it around her shoulders and pulled her tightly against him and then tucked the blanket around them both. "I'm a wolf," he said simply. "What is a blow drier?"

"It's a machine that blows hot air and dries hair fast."

"That would be handy," Taye said solemnly, "if I had hair as long as yours." As beautiful as yours, he added to himself. Maybe she would let him comb it?

The shivers were easing, and Carla seemed relaxed against him. He savored it and her breath on his chest. Ever since he had showed her his wolf she had seemed to trust him more. Strange, he would have thought it would have been the other way around. That had not been his mother's reaction to his father's wolf. But whatever the reason, he welcomed the chance to hold her in his arms. She pushed away too soon. He made himself let her go. Earning her trust might half kill him, but he would do it.

"Warmer now?" he asked briskly. "Let me help you dry your hair, and then we should get to breakfast before it is all gone."

"I can do my hair myself," she said with a touch of her old hauteur.

Taye sighed in inward disappointment, but only nodded. Maybe another time she would allow him to fuss with her hair. Among wolves it was common for them to groom one another and rub up against each other. Not in a sexual way, but just for the comfort of being close. Hugging and rubbing up against another wolf meant they were part of the pack. The boys in the Pack often leaned against each other or put their arms around each other. The humans in town didn't understand it. With so few women it wasn't unknown for men to form physical relationships, and that's what they thought the Pack did. But wolves did not see other men as sexually attractive. They weren't even attracted to women who were mated to another wolf.

Carla's water-darkened hair hung in a single braid to the belt of her jeans. Taye found himself bending slightly to sniff it as he held her jacket for her to slip her arms in. She glared over her shoulder at him. Ah, things were back to normal. Taye grinned and straightened the collar of her jacket before opening the door. Then he paused, face sober.

"I'm going to introduce you to the Pack this morning. You have to remember that most of them are not human. No one will hurt you, though. You will be special to them because you are my mate. You are the Lupa. Okay?"

Her dark hazel eyes narrowed. "I'm not your mate."

So much for her softening to him. "You will be."

She snorted. "Aren't you going to put on some clothes?"

He was wearing sweatpants, which was more than he usually wore. "I've got clothes on. Let's go to breakfast."

The dining room was silent when they got there, more than three dozen men sitting at the tables with an air of expectancy. Normally they would be talking too loud and eating too fast, and wrestling naked on the floor amid howls and laughter. He had given the order last night for everyone to wear clothes until he said different. They seemed to be on their best behavior this morning, because they all were wearing shorts or pants and waited quietly until he had led Carla over to the table at the head of the room before lifting their faces and letting loose a howl of congratulations. It was thunderous and it made him grin proudly. Carla had a frozen look on her face. Shock? Fear? No, he didn't smell fear, only a little anxiety.

The Pack Betas, his lieutenants, came forward. Pete and Des each lowered their heads to sniff Carla's neck politely. She stiffened and tried to pull back. Taye held her still. "This is Pete, and this is Des. They are my Betas."

Pete had come with him to the Bride Fight yesterday, but Des had been left in charge of the den and their surrounding turf. Des sniffed her again. "She's strong," he commented approvingly. "I accept her as my Alpha

Female." He leaned closer to Taye to speak very quietly. "Better feed her up, though. She needs more meat on her bones to get through the winter."

Pete lifted his head to stare hard at Taye. "You haven't had sex with her yet," he announced for the Pack to hear. "She is not yours."

Taye seemed to grow taller, his shoulders broader. "I will take her to bed when the time is right."

Pete spat on the floor between Taye's bare feet. The other wolves were silent except for a few soft growls and whines. "I heard you mean to keep us all on KP, when you have a female right there to do women's work. And you're going to wait until she *allows* you to fuck her? What kind of man are you? Are you an Alpha or a lap dog?"

"Careful, Pete," Taye said casually. "Some Alphas might take that as a challenge."

"Damn straight it's a challenge. I'm claiming the girl and the Alpha place."

Taye laid a soothing hand on Carla's shoulder, stopping her from saying anything. He shook his head sadly. "Pete, don't think I won't kill any man who looks at my mate wrong. I don't want to have to kill you. Show me your throat and we can leave this behind us."

Pete's dark grey eyes shifted over Carla in an insultingly intimate appraisal. "If you want to keep that woman you'll have to kill me, because I'm taking her. I'm not afraid of her boots. She can scream all she wants, but she's not telling *me* no when I want to fuck her. You've turned into a soft little pup, Taye. You'll never kill me."

———

Carla listened to this with a sense of distant horror. Pete was not an ugly man physically, but the way he looked at her and talked to Taye made her feel sick. If he had been the one to win the Bride Fight, last night would have gone horribly differently. Without really meaning to she took a half-step behind Taye.

"Your challenge is accepted," said Taye flatly. "Call the Pack. Let them stand witness."

Pete's smile was hard and smug. "Good. I'll meet you outside."

He and the men in the dining room left. Carla stepped back to Taye's side. "What was that all about?"

"Pete has been on the verge of challenging me for months," he answered after a pause. "I've always been able to back him down before. Today I gave him a chance, but he won't yield."

"I don't understand." And I don't like him, she added silently.

"My uncle told me last year that I was too laid-back for an Alpha. I let Pete get away with too much insolence. I should have done something about it before this. I guess I'll have to take care of it now. Come on, you have to watch."

Carla let him steer her through the dining room to the lobby and outside. There was little breeze, which was good, because it was cold enough to see her breath. Off to one side of what had survived of the asphalt parking lot, men and boys were standing around in their bare feet, crushing the frost-crisp grass. Some of them were no older than fifteen by Carla's estimate. Most of them appeared to be Native American, but some were blond and others brunet. Almost all of them wore only shorts or pants in spite of the low temperature. They turned to watch as Taye led her through the crowd and to the far side of an empty area about thirty feet square. Pete stood facing them from the other side of the square stark naked. Taye stopped her beside the other man he had introduced her to this morning. Des. She thought his name was Des. Taye leaned down to put his mouth against her ear.

"I'm going to kiss you. It's for show. Don't push me away."

His lips were very gentle against hers, his large hand warm on the back of her neck. It was done by the time she got her wits back. She blinked at him while he quickly pulled off his sweats. She gaped at his nudity for only a second before he turned into the big gray wolf she had seen last night. He paced to the center of the square and another wolf, even larger, met him. Pete? Good lord, were they going to fight? She felt the cold air freezing her wet braid, and felt the same sort of icy cold inside.

Des patted her shoulder. "Don't worry. Pete can't take Taye."

The fight lasted only about four or five minutes, but it seemed to go on forever. Half the time Carla couldn't tell which wolf was Taye. The gray bodies writhed together, kicking up clumps of grass and slinging saliva and blood and tufts of fur into the air. Constant growling was broken by occasional yelps. Both were bleeding and limping by the time one wolf clamped his jaws over the throat of another and bit savagely down, shaking his head to break the neck of the loser. The winner stood for a few seconds, his sides heaving, then turned and limped towards Carla.

"See?" whispered Des. "Told ya Taye would win."

A rush of relief bubbled up in Carla, overwhelming her horror at the brutality of the fight. Taye had won and Pete wouldn't rape her. She laid shaking fingers on an unbloodied portion of Taye's gray-furred head. A wave of heat passed pushed her hand up, and Taye stood tall beside her, blood running down from torn-up skin on the back of his left shoulder, over his lower belly from a ragged bite near his navel, down his thigh from a claw scrape. Carla was so horrified she barely noticed he was naked. He slung a heavy arm over her shoulders and swept hard eyes over the dozens of men watching.

"I am Alpha of this Pack, and this is my mate. Is there anyone else who wants to challenge me?"

All the men tilted their heads to the side, chins up, and cast their eyes down. Taye nodded once, satisfied. "Then go about your day, and let everyone you pass know what happened here."

Carla felt more of his weight leaning on her. "Taye, are you—?"

"In a minute," he cut her off in a soft voice. "Des, clean this mess up." Des nodded and went to the dead wolf. Taye watched the men walk away, and when they were a distance off he let her go long enough to pick up his sweatpants and pull them on. "Now we'll go in and eat breakfast, and then we'll go back to our room."

"You're hurt," she protested.

He put his arm around her shoulders again. "But I can't look like it. The Alpha can't show weakness and neither can his mate. So let's go enjoy our breakfast. Don't look like you're hurrying, but don't waste time either, okay? And if you can bear it, please look like you're happy that I won. It will be easier for me if I can lean on you."

Carla almost blurted out that she *was* happy he had won. Taye was a million times better than Pete would have been as a husband. She hadn't felt grateful that Taye had claimed her for his mate until now. But knowing what sort of man she could have spent last night with made her realize how lucky she had been. So she put her arm around his back and walked with him back to the table at the head of the dining room, trying to look like she wasn't supporting so much of his weight. She didn't protest when Taye asked her to bring him some food. She picked the biggest and bloodiest piece of meat on the platter sitting in a covered warming pan on the counter, scooped some oatmeal into a pair of bowls, added a couple apples and went back to the table. Other men were also crowded around tables, some talking quietly, but all watching them avidly.

Taye had propped his chin on his fist and was watching her with a lazy smile. He indicated the space next to him. "Bring your chair over here, mate, so I can flirt with you."

Carla stopped, ready to protest, but then she saw how much of his weight was supported by his elbow on the table, and remembered that he had said he couldn't appear weak. She set the heavy tray on the table and pulled the chair around beside his. When she sat down he immediately wrapped his arm around her shoulders and leaned against her to sniff her neck. She wondered uneasily if that was werewolf foreplay? When his tongue touched the skin under her ear she was sure of it. But with dozens of men watching she couldn't slap him.

"Here, darling," she said stiffly. "Let me cut your meat for you."

His eyes laughed at her. "I'm wounded, not senile."

She smiled back and batted her lashes like a rock star's groupie. "Are you sure?"

He let her go to reach for the fork and knife and managed to control his expression when the muscles of his lower belly seized with pain. "Well, if it would give you pleasure, sweet mate, how can I refuse?"

Carla cut his meat. The blood oozed out of it like his blood was oozing out of him. "Darling," she said pointedly. "Hurry and eat. You need ... I want to, um, go back to bed."

The men—wolves?—around them seemed to prick up their ears, and they weren't shy about watching the Alpha couple. Their tongues were practically hanging out of their mouths while they listened. Taye leaned against her again to nibble her jaw. "Your wish is my command."

Carla stabbed a chunk of meat with more violence than was necessary. "How sweet," she cooed between clenched teeth. "Here, eat some meat."

He accepted it and kissed her fingertips on the knife. "Your fingers are cold. I'll warm you up," he promised, his chin resting on her shoulder. "Then I'll dress you in furs like a Russian princess."

Carla could feel the weak little tremors that passed through him and took more of his weight. "Won't that be nice."

Taye turned breakfast into a mock seduction, but Carla was distressed by how effective it was. Maybe Taye wasn't pretending to seduce her. With every lick and nibble he gave her fingers she felt herself grow warmer and lose a few more of her inhibitions. Maybe he was serious. Good grief, if this was how he made love when he was wounded she had better stay away from him when he was whole. She tried to look natural when they walked out of the dining room with their arms around each other, but the only acting experience she'd had was when she had made a couple of music videos for her debut CD, and she hadn't been very good at that either.

It was a relief when she closed the door to their room and Taye let her go to drag himself to the bathroom. But he looked so weak she went after him and helped him wipe the blood away from his wounds. The one on the back of his shoulder was still bleeding, but the one in his lower belly looked worse, the gouge in his flesh going pretty deep and the edges not meeting. Carla felt like crying.

"Tell me the truth, Taye, how bad is it?"

He was sitting naked on the closed toilet seat with a hand towel barely covering his nakedness. "Well," he said in a voice held tight against the pain. "It's bad, but not so bad that I don't notice the brush of your hair on my … Never mind. Wolves heal fast. I think three days and I'll be 100 percent. Thanks for playing along in the dining room. It's our nature to take advantage of weakness. I don't really want to fight another challenge. If you don't mind, we'll keep it up a few days so I can rest up and heal. The boys will think we're having our honeymoon."

"But…" Carla hesitated. "Pete. How did Pete know we hadn't…"

"He could smell it," Taye replied matter-of-factly. "Wolves can smell that."

"Oh." Carla's voice was very small. "Then won't the others know too? That we haven't, um."

Taye shook his head tiredly. "We'll figure it out. Can you help me to the bed?"

Carla obligingly propped her shoulder under his

and firmly forbade herself to look as the towel slipped off his hips. She let him ease onto the bed and covered him with the blankets, and stood uncertainly by the bed, squeezing her fingers over and over. She couldn't look at Taye. "I wonder … maybe … I mean, you know. Maybe we should—" She waved her hand nervously. "—you know."

Taye's dark eyes blinked sleepily up at her. "Hm?"

Carla took a breath and blurted it out. "Um. We should have sex. So nobody else will challenge you."

She finally peeked at him to find him frowning up at her. "Carla, do you want to have sex with me? Really?"

Her hands waved nervously again. "Well…"

He cut her off with a weary shake of his head. "That's a no. Even if I wasn't as weak as mauled five-day-old kitten I wouldn't take you up on that. Not until you're absolutely sure that you want me. We'll talk about it again when I'm stronger."

"Oh. Okay." Why didn't she feel more relieved by his refusal? Disappointment was not the right emotion to be feeling right now.

"Your clothes are all bloody," he murmured, on the edge of sleep. "Go wash up and put on one of my shirts from the drawer there. Then come lie down with me."

She was glad he was going to be okay. She was

really glad Pete hadn't killed him. And she was glad he had refused her half-hearted offer of sex. Of course she was. Very glad. She stripped off her bloodstained shirt and jeans and washed before putting on a thick white T-shirt that came down to her thighs. It looked like the fabric was a very fine hand-knit. Did they have the machinery to make knit fabric these days? Someone must have spent hours knitting this shirt. Careful not to jar him or even touch him, she lay close to the edge of the bed. But he tugged on her braid until she scooted closer to him. Half an hour later Carla drifted into sleep, warm for the first time since she'd gotten out of bed that morning.

CHAPTER FIVE

Carla woke feeling almost too warm. Taye was like a human space heater. She looked over her shoulder at him and saw that he was still deeply asleep. Good. He probably needed all the sleep he could get. Maybe she should lie back down too. But the sun was coming thru a little gap in the curtains, and she had a snatch of a melody running through her mind, with a few words. She had learned a long time ago that when an idea for a song poked at her it was best to pay attention. The title for the song was already set in her mind: "Sleeping With The Wolf." She carefully eased out from under Taye's arm and tucked the covers back around him.

It was warmer than it had been this morning, but still chilly for wearing only a T-shirt. The blanket Taye had wrapped around her before they went to breakfast was draped over one of the chairs at the table. A really thick robe and big fuzzy slippers would be nice. She picked up the blanket and put it around her shoulders before getting her purse and digging inside for her notebook and pen. It took a while to find what she wanted, since she had just about everything in her bag including her knitting. She paused to wonder where she could get more yarn. Wool socks would be nice to have this winter. She got her notebook and settled down in the chair where the sun was streaming and began to play with the song in her head.

———

Taye woke a while later, feeling the pain of his wounds and the loss of Carla's warmth. He saw her right away, though, sitting in a beam of sunlight. The room seemed warm to him, but she had a blanket wrapped around her shoulders and tucked under her crossed legs. Her hair was loose down her back, soaking up the sun. She was humming softly and writing in a book. She would hum the same thing over and over, then pause to write in her book, then sing a little under her breath.

One bright morning got on a plane,
That's the day the world ended.
Feels like I've gone insane,
My world can't be mended.

———

The wolf chose me,
But I'm not sleeping with the wolf.
The wolf won me,
But I'm not sleeping with the wolf.
The wolf saved me,
Should I be sleeping with the wolf?
If he loves me,
Then I'll love him,
And I'll be sleeping with the wolf.

———

The plane went down in a field,
Of grass and death and dying.
My walk for help my fate sealed,
I was fooled by farmers lying.
Hmmm hmmm…

Taye let her low voice seep through him. It soothed him almost as much as her scent lingering on the pillow beside him. "If he loves me, then I'll love him…" Would she love him? He loved her. She was his mate. She was the most valuable person in his world. Her sadness and her fear tore him up inside worse than anything Pete's teeth and claws had done to his body. Alpha wolves were generally domineering even with their mates. Most would have demanded sex last night, or at least coaxed for it. But he simply hadn't been able to do that to her. He had fallen in love with her at first sight. Had he told her he loved her, would she have believed him? Probably not. His mate was prickly. He had to show her he loved her. Right now she didn't look sad or frightened. She was focused on something he wasn't part of. She put down her pen and book and held her hands strangely, still humming, like she was … playing a guitar. Sure, she was making music. He could get her a guitar. Dane Overdahl collected all kinds of stuff from the Times Before. So did Mr. Gray down at the library. Maybe they could make a trade.

A knock sounded on the door. Carla jumped, but Taye knew it was Des. "Let him in," he said.

Carla's looked at him questioningly.

"It's Des." Taye pulled himself up carefully to sit with his back against the headboard fastened to the wall. The wound on the back of his shoulder protested slightly. "Let him in."

Carla arranged the blanket so it covered more

of her and went to the door. Humans had a positive fetish about covering their bodies. It would be a shock to Carla when she realized that the Pack mostly went naked inside the den. His mother had commanded that they all wear at least some clothing in the den. Would Carla also command that?

Des stepped in, giving Carla a polite head dip that made his long hair spill over his chest before grabbing a chair and putting it by the bed and slouching in it. "Hey, Chief." He sniffed the air. "You okay? Not up to mating yet?"

Taye watched his mate's cheeks flush with color. "Doing pretty good, Des, but some things shouldn't be rushed."

"Ah." Des nodded wisely. "Take your word for it. You slept right through lunch. I came by a couple hours ago, and the two of you were dead to the world. Supper'll be ready in a half hour. You want me to bring you something?"

Taye remembered Carla's revulsion over the rare meat last night. "Why don't you walk Carla down to the kitchen? She likes her steak a little more dead than we do. She can fix hers herself and bring supper back for both of us."

Carla grabbed her clothes and went into the bathroom to get changed. Taye spoke softly. "Des, my mate gets real cold. Get that wood stove fixed up in here for her, huh? The one we had for my mother. I think we put it out in the shed. And send a couple boys out to find her a guitar. We got enough hides to trade. Dane Overdahl or Mr. Gray might have something like that. Any signs of trouble in the Pack over the challenge?"

"Nope. Pete's not much of a loss. Some of the boys don't understand why you would wait to take your mate. I guess I don't either. None of my business," Des hastened to add. "Just seems like being so close to her all the time and not mating her would be hard."

Taye closed his eyes to inhale Carla's scent from the bed. "Someday when you find your mate you'll understand. A woman as precious as your mate deserves special care. A man has to put his mate first. And, Des—" He opened his eyes to fix them on his lieutenant. "—Stick close to her while she's getting supper ready and walk her back here. I don't want any of the boys to get the wrong idea about her."

"Will do." Des got up from the chair as Carla came out of the bathroom and put the folded blanket on the couch. "Ready, Lupa?"

Taye shook his head. "Wait outside a minute, Des. Carla, come over here, okay?"

Carla waited until the door closed behind Des before moving close to the bed. She looked wary.

"What?"

"When you go out there everyone will know we haven't mated. But I want them to smell me on you."

Carla's eyes got big and she backed a step away. "You're hurt. You said—"

Taye laughed, although her reluctance hurt. "We won't make love right now, sweetheart. Just a kiss. So they'll know you're mine."

She came back, looking uncertain, but smelling … curious? He wasn't sure exactly what her scent said, but it wasn't fear. "Just a kiss?"

"Yeah." He rearranged the covers over his hips to hide his body's eagerness. By the way her pulse jumped his efforts weren't entirely successful.

"Looks like you're feeling a lot better," she said pointedly.

Taye wondered if that was an accusation. "Not well enough to do what I'd really like to," he said honestly, with his best smile. "Sit down so I can kiss you. We shouldn't keep Des waiting."

They were both a little awkward trying to turn their bodies to face each other without straining Taye's wounds. Taye put his large hands on her delicate face to pull her lips against his. She was rigid for a minute, her hands fluttering helplessly before settling lightly on his upper arms. Taye could feel her uncertainty in her stiffness. He delicately probed at the seam of her lips with the tip of his tongue and after a hesitation she opened her mouth. Wonder and excitement flooded him when his tongue glided against hers and his kiss turned from tentative to hotly demanding. One of his hands went beneath her hair to cup the back of her neck and pull her harder against him. He felt her hands clench on his biceps and began the torturous task of letting her go. He refused to frighten her off. He *would not* make her hate him. He stared down at her flushed face and tried to find the words to apologize, but she put her hands around the back of his neck and pulled his face down, and kissed him with as much hunger as he had kissed her. Her scent held traces of feminine desire, and if her hand hadn't grazed the wound on his back he might have forgotten about Des waiting in the hall, forgotten his empty belly and the fact that he was too weak to mate with her and dragged her under the covers. He let her go, and made himself lean back against the headboard, his eyes closed and his breathing shakier than it had ever been in his life.

"I'm so sorry!" she said in a strangled voice. "I'll go get supper!"

Then she bolted out of the room, leaving him wondering what she was thinking. Was she sorry she had kissed him? He wasn't. He was planning to do it a lot more.

———

Carla was so dazed by the kiss she almost ran into the man talking to Des in the hall. "Oh, sorry," she blurted. She had hurt Taye by grabbing his shoulder. The kiss had made her forget all about his wounds. He had taken his large warm hands away and leaned back practically groaning in pain. Carla cringed inside. She hadn't meant to hurt him. Of course, she hadn't meant to kiss him either. Boy, he could kiss. Holy cow, could he kiss!

Des nodded at her. The other man sniffed and smiled. Carla glared uncomfortably. Could they actually smell that she and Taye had kissed? Her panties were wet. Maybe they could smell that? What was wrong with her? Taye was a killer. But ... He could have raped her last night instead of giving her space. And he could really kiss ... She walked down the hall, immersed in lines for the next verse of her song. "*The wolf kissed me...*"

Des said a something quietly to the other man before following half a step behind her into the empty dining hall, and directed her into the kitchen with a nod to the open door. The kitchen was pretty good-sized, with an indoor brick trough under a half-open window that was apparently a fire pit, and a row of big metal sinks along another wall. There was a man already there, or actually a boy, since she didn't think he was older than sixteen or seventeen, laying out dozens of steaks on the metal island. The designated cook for the day? He was young but already tall and muscular, and in a few years he would be as handsome as Taye. He wore a leather apron that covered him from collarbone to knee. His long thick black hair was in a ponytail that ended right over his tailbone. She stared for a moment at his bare backside visible between the edges of the apron. Clothes were apparently optional, but at least he had the good sense to wear an apron in the kitchen.

"Hi," Carla said brightly. "I'm Carla."

The young cook watched her blankly with vivid blue eyes as she took a small steak and put it on the grill that was propped over the coals of the fire pit, and selected a second steak, the thickest and largest one on the counter, for Taye. She was sure the cook wanted to say something to her, but he kept his mouth shut, just looking at her sullenly from under thick black brows. Maybe he didn't like her coming in and taking his steaks? Maybe he didn't like the fact that she and Taye hadn't ... Carla sniffed at herself. All she could smell was the cooking meat. Her stomach growled.

"What?" she finally said after enduring several

minutes under his intense stare.

"Is it true you're not going to cook for us?"

Des growled, and the teenager tipped his head back in that disturbing gesture of showing his throat. "Watch your mouth and show the Lupa some respect," Des snarled.

Carla swallowed. "I asked, Des."

"It's not his place to question you, Lupa."

Carla flipped her steak. "Well, maybe I should answer anyway." She waved the large sharp grilling fork at the young man, making him step smoothly back. He must be one of the wolves. Humans just didn't move with that kind of feral grace. "I'm willing to take my turn at cooking, but I don't plan to do it every day. Where I come from we don't cook over open fires, and just because a person is female doesn't make her a cook. But," she added prudently, "that's up to Taye." Speaking of whom … She slapped the second steak on the grill. "What's your name?"

He rattled off a long string of meaningless syllables. At her blank look he translated. "Blue Sky at Midday. Call me Sky." He glanced at her steak with warning. "Your meat is burnt."

She pulled it off the fire and smiled with satisfaction. "No, it's cooked. Just the way I like it." She couldn't help but laugh at his horror. "See? You don't want me cooking your steak."

She took Taye's steak off the grill. It was lightly browned on both sides, hopefully just the way he liked it. Sky showed her where the potatoes were baking in the coals at the far end of the fire pit and the pot of carrots hanging above them. She piled a tray with food for the two of them and when she lifted it she let out a grunt at the weight. Des waved a hand at the dining room. A few men were beginning to gather. One of them came over. Like the other men in the dining hall he was stark naked. Carla focused on his face, not letting her eyes go lower. He looked familiar. He had been with them when they walked home from the Bride Fight. Jay? Jason? He took the tray and carried it for her back to Taye's room. Des led the way briskly, his too big cotton pants fluttering with his speed, but the closer they came to Taye the more reluctant Carla was. How could she face Taye? She had flung herself so deeply into the kiss she had hurt him. Maybe he thought she had done it for revenge?

The door of room 121 opened before they got there and a couple men came out. They stared at Carla and held the door open for Jay to carry the tray in before going off down the hallway. Jay set the tray down on the table and he and Des left. Carla had to steel herself to look at Taye. But she didn't see him right away. The

81

room seemed full of men. Her eyes skipped over them, trying to not see their nakedness, and found the old-fashioned pot-bellied stove sitting past the window. Taye was crouched beside it, feeding it small pieces of wood. Tears came to her eyes. She was always cold, and winter hadn't even started yet. Taye had said something about a stove to help her keep warm, and here it was. Even after she had hurt him he took care of her.

He stood up and turned to face her with a small smile. She let her eyes slide down his bare brown body and sighed with relief when she saw that he was wearing cut-offs. The gouge below his belly button still looked angry and raw, but the gash on his thigh was definitely healing. He held out a hand to her and she went to him. It felt good when he pulled her face to his chest and kissed the top of her head.

"The stove is for you," he murmured. "I hate to think of you being cold."

Carla forced the tears back. "Thank you." She meant it, and she wanted to show her gratitude but wasn't sure how. Strange. A day ago she would have bitten him rather than let him hug her. She suppressed the impulse to kiss him. There were other men in the room, all looking at them with interest. The urge to run her hands over his muscled chest was so strong she backed out of his embrace and stood before the small fire with her hands spread to the heat.

She smiled at all the men, and let her eyes linger on Taye. "Thank you. This is wonderful. Thank you all."

The men—there were only three of them, not the crowd she had imagined—all smiled happily back. One of them wore a carpenter's apron around his waist that he was putting tools into. It looked ridiculous, considering he was naked. "We'll start collecting more wood, Lupa. By the time the snow comes we'll have enough to keep you warm all winter."

This was prairie land. Where would the wood come from? Carla hadn't seen very many trees when she and Lisa had walked to find help for the … Plane crash survivors! She had been so wrapped up in her own problems that she had forgotten them. "Taye!"

He came quickly at the urgent note in her voice. "Yes, sweetheart?"

"The plane! There were other survivors who need help. Oh, God! I forgot all about them. We have to help them!"

"The plane?" Taye blinked. "You truly fell out of the sky? I thought Ray was only saying that." Now he shook his head. "Where did you fall, sweetheart?"

"It was west of here. Me and Lisa walked south for a few hours before we found a road. County Road 30, the sign said. Then we walked east for almost two days until we got to the farmers." Carla wanted to say something bitter about the farmers who had sold them to Ray, but suppressed it and went on. "We told them about the plane crash, but they pretty much ignored us. Maybe they went to the plane crash after…"

Taye shook his head. "I doubt it. The Odessa farmers wouldn't go so far from their homes. But we're wolves and we go where we please." He looked at the men. "Find Des and send him to me."

The door opened. "No need to send for me, I'm here, Chief," said Des. "What'cha need?"

"Put together a small scouting mission. Take five of the boys and send them out to find the place my mate fell. Sweetheart, can you tell us where you struck Highway 30?"

"Well, not long after we came to the road we passed through a ghost town. It might have been called Lexington. I think that's what the sign said."

"Find the place and see if there is anyone who needs help," Taye instructed. "Bring them here."

Des slanted a doubtful look at Carla. "If you say so, Chief. Sure."

Taye smiled a small sly smile. "Sweetheart, how many females were on the plane?"

"Grown-ups? I don't know. Maybe thirty-five? Forty? And a couple kids, I think, and some teenagers."

All the men gasped. "Can I go?" the man in the apron whined to Des. "I gotta see that many women in one place. Maybe we can find mates."

"But… " Carla swallowed. "Some of them died in the crash. And some of them are hurt."

Des nodded briskly. "Then we need to hurry."

"Yeah," said one of the other men darkly. "We have to find them before somebody else does and steals them from us."

"Get some supper," Des ordered. "And meet me in the rec room in twenty minutes. You three can come, and I'll get a couple more."

As they hurried out Carla called, "Wear clothes unless you want to scare them to death! Gosh," she said to Taye. "If Lisa and me had found you first we could have gotten help a lot sooner."

Taye put his arm around her shoulders. "We'll do our best to help them. Let's eat. I'm starved."

Carla let him move her over to the table. "Our food must be cold by now. I'm sorry."

"It's all right." He seated her and paused before going to his chair to brush his fingertips down the arm of her blouse. "I know humans wear clothes in the winter because they'd be cold otherwise, but why do they wear clothes when it's hot?"

Carla paused in cutting her steak to stare at him

85

suspiciously. "Are you teasing me?"

"A little. Wolves prefer to be naked."

"I noticed," she muttered, stuffing a piece of cold steak into her mouth.

"Does it bother you so much?"

"I don't like seeing men I barely know naked. It's gross."

"What about me?" he asked curiously. "You look at me when I'm wearing clothes, but you don't when I'm not. Why?"

"Because," Carla began, feeling the blush roll up her face. "Good lord. How's your steak? Not too well done, I hope?"

"It's perfect. Carla, why? Am I ugly?"

She set her knife down with a thump. "You know you're not!"

"No, I don't. I've never had a mate before, so I didn't care if women thought I was handsome or ugly. But I care what you think."

Carla found herself looking away from him and realized she did this a lot. And she knew why. She just wasn't sure it was a good idea to tell him that all his hard muscles covered with smooth brown skin made her want to pet him. "You are very handsome," she said, studying her plate to keep her eyes busy with something besides him. "In my time women would have been all over you. You would have had your pick of the hundreds following you everywhere you went."

"Would you have followed me?"

Carla swallowed more cold steak. "No." She had too much pride for that, but if he were the friend of a friend or someone she met at the studio she might have tried to let him know she was interested in knowing him better. "Eat up. I slaved over that steak for you."

He obeyed, but Carla wondered what he would say next. "Tell me about the plane, sweetheart. What is it like to fly?"

Carla shrugged. "I don't know. I flew a lot the past couple years. Some people are afraid of flying. I never was, but I can understand it now." She fixed her attention on arranging her carrots in neat piles. Even now the memory of the crash made her stomach lurch. "I've never been so afraid in my life," she whispered.

Taye reached across the table to smooth the back of his knuckles over her cheek. "I'm glad you're all right."

Carla nodded and began eating her supper, hoping her stomach would settle down. Taye watched her and made sure she ate every bite. He ate everything on his plate before gathering their empty plates on to the tray and putting them out in the hall. Just like last night, he leaned on the door and looked at her. Was that only last night? Twenty-four hours ago she had been terrified he would rape her. How could she have changed her mind so fast?

"How are you feeling?" she blurted.

He looked down and passed a hand over his flat belly, probing cautiously at the wound there. "Still pretty sore. The sleep helped, but not enough so I can make love to you tonight."

"Oh, goo—I mean, we need to be careful."

He looked disappointed. "You know I won't force you, right?"

"Yes." And she did. He wouldn't need to anyway. This morning Pete had opened her eyes to what kind of mate she could have had. And Taye was trying to make her happy. Or at least comfortable. She could bear it. Maybe even enjoy it. Someday. "Do you mind if I pull my chair in front of the stove?"

"I'll do it."

"You're hurt. I'll do it."

"You're awfully stubborn, mate," he observed, pulling his own chair next to hers in front of the stove.

She plopped down. "It came in handy while building a music career," she huffed.

"You sang and played music to earn money?" Taye guessed.

"Yes, and I was getting pretty popular at it too. I was in Minneapolis for a show, and then I got on the plane to go to Denver to sing for a crowd of fifty thousand people. That's where I was going when … I guess my career is over now."

———

Career was like a foreign word to Taye. Men did what they could these days. Their wives and families helped them. Farmers grew the grain that Dane Overdahl's mill ground into flour. Other farmers raised milk cows and made cheese and butter for trade. Ranchers raised cattle for meat and sheep for wool and horses for riding and pulling wagons. The mill west of town bought wool fleeces and spun the wool into thread to weave fabric for clothing and other needs. He and his pack hunted meat and tanned hides that they traded for what they needed. A couple of times a year the traveling traders came through Kearney to sell outrageously expensive goods that couldn't be locally produced. Boats came up the Platte River to sell things too. They also passed along news, carried mail, and sometimes allowed other travelers to join them for protection. Some of the traders also told stories and performed music, and the listeners would thank them by buying meals and providing places for them to sleep. It was hard to imagine a woman going from place to place to sing, especially one who didn't have a husband

and family to protect her. How could she keep herself safe? The Times Before were as strange to him as the world of a science fiction novel would be to her.

She looked very sad right now, almost tearful. He couldn't bear that, so he reached and gripped her hand. "Sweetheart, you never answered me. Do you think I'm ugly?"

She squirmed in her chair but didn't jerk her hand away. "No. I said you are handsome."

"Did I frighten you when I kissed you?"

"No."

"But you were sorry. You said so."

Her eyes flashed over to his face for a moment before dropping again. "I was sorry. I *am* sorry. I didn't mean to hurt you. It was an accident."

"Sweetheart, what are you talking about?"

Taye held his breath when she looked at him again. Her eyes gleamed with tears. She was so beautiful. He reached his free hand to touch her cheek where the tear would fall. He waited for it, but she tilted her head up and blinked, somehow managing to force the tears back. Awfully stubborn. He found he admired stubborn women.

"When I grabbed your shoulder. When we were kissing. I grabbed you where you were injured by Pete. I hurt you. But I didn't mean to."

"That?" Taye smothered a relieved laugh. "That barely hurt at all. It's a good thing it happened, though."

Now she did jerk her hand away, and he let her.

"Sweetheart, I was ready to forget that I promised to not force you. Another minute and I would have … I would have… " He flicked his fingers at her blouse. "Those are the only clothes you have, right? Well, another minute of kissing you, and they would have been rags because I wouldn't have been too careful taking them off you."

Her mouth and eyes were wide. Her hands clenched around the edges of her blouse, holding them together as if he was about to tear it off her right now. "Taye, don't you dare wreck my clothes!"

Excitement was driving his blood frantically through him, and he wasn't even touching her! She was challenging him, and his nature demanded he dominate her. In an effort to calm himself he smiled teasingly. "You humans are entirely too attached to your clothes. I'll get you more."

"Good," she said sharply. "These are getting rank. I've got dried blood on them. And this is the second day straight I've worn these pantie—these clothes. I need to wash them."

"Every time I tear something I'll replace it," he promised with a grin. "What's a pantie?"

Carla glared. "Very funny! As if you don't know."

Taye shrugged his one uninjured shoulder. He really didn't know. Clothes weren't important to wolves, and women's clothes were just plain foreign. From her reaction a pantie must be an intimate garment. He examined her with interest, wondering what she wore under the blouse and jeans. She released her grip on her blouse, and the glare softened, but only slightly.

"Honestly, Taye, I can't wear the same clothes every day."

"I have a couple T-shirts and more pants," he offered. "But now that we have the stove, isn't warm enough for—"

"No!" she shouted. "Good lord, Taye, you're making me crazy!"

He wondered what the Pack thought of her shout. "Sweetheart, I can hear you just fine. You can wash your clothes in the bathtub tonight and wrap up in the blanket while your clothes dry."

"It will take longer than a couple hours for my clothes to dry. It would be better for me to have a couple changes of clothes," she pointed out more calmly.

"All right. I'll send some of the boys to pick up a few things for you."

Her eyes were disbelieving. "If you think I'll let some strange guys—wolves—pick out my clothes—"

She snorted. "Uh-uh. No way."

"All right," he said again, mildly. "In a few days when I'm feeling better we'll go into Kearney and get you some things. For tonight, if you insist on wearing clothes to bed, you can wear one of my T-shirts and a pair of shorts. But under the covers you'll be warm. You won't need clothes."

"Taye." Somehow she turned his name into three agonized syllables. He liked it. "I'm not ready for that yet, okay? I need to wear something to bed. So do you. Please."

He slanted a feral smile at her. "Not yet? But someday?"

She sighed, looking torn between fear and embarrassment. "Do I really have a choice? I mean, I know you said you would wait 'til I'm ready—"

"I will wait," he cut her off, his voice emphatic. "I won't force you." His voice dropped into a wolf's growl. "But I'll do what I can to tempt you. I won't hurt you. Ever. You're my mate. I want you to scream my name when I'm inside you. With pleasure, not hate, not pain."

She stared, helplessly transfixed by the way his eyes shimmered wolf-gold as they caressed her. "Oh," she breathed. She tingled between her legs, and she saw his nostrils flare as he inhaled. Boy, did she need a clean pair of panties. And a cold shower.

"Sweetheart," he groaned. His hands clenched the arms of his chair, knuckles showing white. "I love the way you smell. I'm not well enough to do much, but I want to play with you. Come here so I can take off your shirt." His eyes glowed hotly when they ran over her. "Slip off your pants. Let me touch you."

Carla tried to control her breathing. He was tempting, and she was aroused by just his words. He hadn't even touched her and she was wet. "No, Taye. I don't want to hurt you."

"I'm hurting now."

"I don't think touching me will make you hurt less. Maybe a cold shower will help."

He leaned his head back with his eyes clenched shut. "Please, sweetheart. Please. Let me touch you. I'll stop when you want."

The Alpha who killed men and commanded a pack of werewolves sounded just like a high school boy trying to sweet talk his date into the back of his pickup. She hesitantly undid her belt buckle. She was stuck here in this future world, and she belonged to Taye. So far he had treated her as well as he could. It was inevitable that they would have sex someday. Wasn't it better to ease into it? A little kissing here, a little petting there, before having full-out sex?

She undid the button of her jeans and slid a look at Taye. His head still leaned back against his chair, but his eyes watched her fingers hungrily.

"Don't look!" she said involuntarily.

He closed his eyes. "Come here, then, so I can feel you."

When Carla stood up and turned so she was facing him, his arm snaked out and looped around her waist. He kept his eyes closed when he dragged her closer. She had to stand so his knee was between her legs. Her breasts were just at the level of his face. His free hand came up to caress them through her shirt. With his arm around her waist he made her sit on his knee. He inhaled gently against her throat and groaned.

"Don't hurt yourself," she said sharply.

His eyes burned into hers. "I feel no pain. Take off your shirt."

"No."

"Why not?"

"I don't want you to look at me."

"Only the Lupa can deny the Alpha and get away with it." Taye made a production of closing his eyes. "I'll let you get away with it if you will let me touch you where ever I want."

Carla thought about it. "Okay."

"Stand up," he ordered huskily. When she had

obeyed his hands stroked over her breasts and down to her thighs, then searched for her zipper. He pulled it down and his fingers wandered over the elastic of her panties' waistband. The muscles in her lower belly clenched in anticipation, but he moved back up, sliding his hands under her blouse to cup her breasts through her bra.

"Kiss me, mate," he murmured.

She did, leaning over and putting her hands on the arms of his chair to brace herself away from his wounds. Somewhere in the middle of his hot, drugging kisses his hands left her breasts and slid inside her jeans. He petted the silk of her panties and learned the shape of her hips and mound. She felt like a new frontier that he was exploring in excruciating detail. She shoved her jeans down her hips to give his large hands more room. His hand moved purposefully into her panties, navigating through soft pubic hair to her slit. He stroked and petted while she bit her lip to control her breathing.

"You're wet." His growl sounded delighted. "You want me."

For answer she pushed her jeans further down and raised one knee to prop her foot on the edge of his chair. "Keep your eyes closed," she commanded.

"They're closed, sweetheart, but I don't like orders.

Remember that."

"Whatever," she said impatiently, wiggling her hips so one of his fingers slipped a fraction of an inch inside her. "Oh!"

Taye sniffed audibly. "You like that. You want more?"

"Uh-huh."

He pushed one finger deep inside her, then took his fingers away to slide one in his mouth. "I like the way you taste."

"Are you going to just tease me?"

"No, sweetheart, I'm going to give you everything you want. Hold onto my shoulder and let me know what you like."

She liked everything he did to her. Each time his finger went deep the heel of his hand brushed over her clitoris. She gripped his uninjured shoulder hard and urged him on with little gasps until her orgasm flooded her. Her legs turned to rubber and she collapsed on to his knee with her forehead pressed to his chest. As her pleasure waned, her embarrassment grew. Taye removed his hand from between her legs and licked his finger clean.

"Sweetheart, are you all right?"

"Fine. Um, did I hurt you?"

"No. Can I open my eyes now?"

"Just a sec." She forced her wet-noodle legs to hold her weight and pulled her jeans back up and fastened them. "Okay."

He looked hard at her face. "What's wrong? Didn't you like that?"

Carla stared at his shoulder. The finger marks from where she had held onto him were fading. "Well, yeah. That's the problem. I hardly know you, and I let you do that to me."

"I'm your mate," he said simply. "There's nothing wrong with what we did."

Carla supposed not. She had certainly enjoyed herself. They were married. Or the wolf Pack equivalent of married. Still, it felt wrong. The front of his sweatpants showed that he had not enjoyed himself quite as much as she had. Maybe she should…?

"Nah," said Taye, reading her mind, or at least the direction of her gaze. "I'm good. I can wait a while until you're willing to go the whole distance. Shouldn't be too long, I hope?"

"You're still hurt," she pointed out shakily. "We'll talk about it later. I have to wash my clothes, and I need a shower."

"The water will be ice cold," Taye warned.

"Good."

When Carla had gotten off his knee and collected some of his clothes and retreated to the bathroom, Taye got up and went to the door of their room. As he expected, the hallway was full of young wolves sniffing the air appreciatively. Taye folded his arms over his bare chest and said mildly, "The Lupa wouldn't like it if she knew we'd had an audience."

Sky and the other young wolves looked abashed.

"And I don't like it either," Taye continued, still mild, but with a growl edging the words.

Abashment turned to fear. The pups quickly exposed their throats.

"Go to bed."

They scurried down the hall. Satisfied that his Pack still held him in proper awe, Taye went back into his room.

Later that evening, after Carla had washed her clothes in the tub and hung them over the shower rail, she put on the longest of his T-shirts and smallest of his cut-off shorts and crawled into bed. She fell asleep quickly in spite of the long nap they had taken earlier. He went into the bathroom and examined the clothing hanging on the rail. He recognized the blouse, jeans, and socks, but the other two items were strange. They looked flimsy. The fabric was bright pink, soft and slippery, edged with lace. These then, must be her pantie. He had petted them tonight while caressing his mate. Their shape allowed him to guess how she would wear them. He hoped that someday soon she would model them for him. He liked the idea of her wearing them and nothing else while he … Already aching with longing, he cut that mental image off. His shower was ice cold but didn't force his erection to retreat. He used his own hand in a brisk business-like manner to ease himself. To imagine it was Carla's hand would be like cheating.

After he dried off, he put his shorts on and got into bed with his mate. He was healing fast, but not quickly enough. He lay on his side, his chest pressed against her back. Under the covers her thighs were mostly bare. He allowed his fingertips to stroke up and down the warm flesh on the outside of her thigh from her knee to the edge of the shorts. She was so soft. And she smelled so good, even with the sharp odor of soap overlaying her natural scent.

And, best of all, she had promised that someday she would lie here without his shorts in the way of his hands. Taye drifted to sleep wondering how soon someday would come.

CHAPTER SIX

The room was cold when Carla woke. She should get up and put some wood in the stove, but it was so cozy in bed. Taye was a solid warmth beside her, and she turned to peer down at him. He was lying on his back with one arm thrown up over his head and the other resting on her thigh. The room was just light enough for her to see the column of his throat leading to his broad shoulders and muscled chest. The blankets were pushed down below his pecs, and she had to admit he had a fine physique. How had she ended up with such a handsome man? She had known other buff, handsome men, like those dancers in her video, but Taye was different. He was ... hers. She was reaching a tentative hand toward his chest when he made a sound. She jerked her hand back and shot her eyes to his face. He was smiling at her like a naughty boy.

"Feel free to pet me," he invited.

"I better add some wood to the stove," she squeaked, throwing back the covers. Memories of what his hands had done to her last night flooded her face with crimson.

His hand squeezed her thigh. "Carla, don't leave me. Please touch me." He folded his arms and tucked his hands under his head. His biceps bulged in that position, drawing her eyes to them. "Anywhere. I won't touch back, I promise. Not right now, anyway."

She hesitated before pulling the covers back over herself. He had kept his promise not to look at her last night and had given her an orgasm without asking for one in return. She had barely touched him last night, and she'd wanted to. "I'm not sure this is a good idea. I don't want to hurt you."

"My back and my leg are good. My stomach is better, but not well enough for more than petting. I don't expect to be able to make love to you this morning. The spirit is willing, but the flesh is weak. So pet me, sweetheart, please."

Making love with Taye was inevitable. Last night she had decided she could bear it, and he had taught

her that he could make her body respond. "Okay…"
Carla hadn't felt this kind of guilty excitement since she
was in high school and Derek had talked her into the
back of his pickup after the homecoming game. Which
was stupid. She was a grown woman of twenty-five,
and Taye was her husband. Mate. Whatever. She barely
grazed his cheek with her fingertips, and then trailed
them down his throat to his collarbone and over the
hard curve of muscle to his nipple. He made a sound
like a cat purring. She jerked her hand away, staring
wide-eyed at his face.

"No, sweetheart," he crooned. "Don't stop now."

She tucked her hair behind her ear. "Your skin is
so warm," she murmured, laying both hands over his
pecs and caressing lightly. Her hair fell to slither over
his chest. She quickly moved to scoop it back, but he
smiled and shook his head.

"I love your hair. Can I comb it for you?"

"Maybe another time," she whispered, putting
it firmly behind her ear again. His shoulders were
muscular, his biceps bulging, his chest like a living
sculpture that responded to every touch. She slid her
caress to the edge of the blanket and back up, scraping
her nails lightly over his nipples, and enjoyed having all
that powerful muscle jump under her hands. Since he
seemed to react to that, she bent and touched the very

tip of her tongue to his tight little nipple, and smiled at the ragged noise he made. She licked a path over his chest to his throat and under his ear and paused there to nibble his earlobe.

"I like that," he told her huskily with a feral smile that made her blood run faster because it made him look so dangerous. And yet, under her hands he was tamed. Maybe. With a single powerful twist he put her on her back and wedged his groin between her thighs.

He took her left hand in his to examine her fingertips. "Calluses," he noted thoughtfully. "Only here."

"From playing the guitar," she told him, smoothing her other hand over his chest, teasing him with her fingers.

Taye held her hand to his lips and kissed her palm. He pressed the inside of her wrist to his nose and inhaled like a connoisseur testing the bouquet of a fine wine. "You smell divine. Let me taste."

He licked her palm and then sucked her middle finger into his mouth. Heat bloomed in Carla, and she felt her brain turn to Jell-O as she pushed her hips up against him. He groaned. "Oh!" She breathed raggedly. "Fire!" She jerked her hand away from him. "Gotta put the fire out … I mean, put wood on the fire!" She squirmed out from under him, fell out of bed in a sprawl of flailing limbs, and scrambled up to lunge for the small woodpile under the window. She blindly tossed some in to the stove and fled to the bathroom. "Gotta get dressed now!" she called toward the bed. Dimly, she was aware she was behaving like a fool, but she had to get away. Taye was just too tempting. If she had stayed she would have had his shorts off him and ravished his beautiful body. "Breakfast! Get up, it's time for breakfast!"

———

Taye lay back on the bed and clamped Carla's pillow over his face to smother his laughter. Here he was, the twenty-four-year-old Alpha of a wolf pack, giggling like a little boy all because he was able to rattle his normally calm, cool mate. But he couldn't help it. Carla without her glacial disdain was adorable. And the laughter barely pulled at his lower belly. Maybe tonight he would be able to consummate his mating. He lifted the blanket and sighed at the peak rising in the front of his cut-off sweatpants. His spirit was willing and his flesh looked pretty strong too. He put Carla's pillow aside and got up and smoothed the blankets back into place. Then he went to the stove and put the fire to rights. He stood by the table, waiting for his mate to come back out, and while he waited he planned exactly, to the smallest detail, what he would do to his mate tonight.

Carla kept a prim distance from Taye on the way to breakfast, and since he was trying to get his body to cool down he allowed it. She was back to being coolly disdainful. He refused even to think of how he could wrap her hair around his wrist to drag her closer and melt the disdain. That was for later.

That morning's breakfast was the best meal he'd had with his mate. Supper the first night had been tense with his lust and her fear. Breakfast yesterday had been tense with his pain and her anxiety. Supper last night had been better for both of them, but not this almost relaxed near flirting. He would make some teasing comment, and she would pause, then fire some cold retort back that made him want to laugh. He would casually brush her fingers with his, and she would sometimes clench her hand into a fist and snatch it back with a glare, and sometimes she would blush a little and peek at him through her lashes. Tease, he wanted to say, but she might go back to being Glacier Carla, so he didn't. He wanted Volcano Carla tonight. His plan included ways to thaw her out, and he hoped she made him work for it. That would be fun.

They sat at the head table alone since Des was still out with the scouts looking for the crash survivors.

He would have to name a second beta soon to take Pete's place. He would discuss it with Des when he got back. And Carla should be involved. She was the Alpha Female, and in his absence she would rule the Pack, if she was able to stand against trouble. He remembered her pointy-toed boot self-defense and grinned. Yes, she could hold her own.

He called some of the men he would consider for beta to the table and introduced them to Carla. Taye could see Carla steeling herself against cringing when they leaned close to touch her hair and inhale her scent. She didn't understand that they were Pack and that they all needed touch and scent to bond. He told the story of the attempted woman-stealing and how she had single-handedly defended herself with no weapon but her boots. He told it casually, with an amused smile, but he made sure they all knew how proud he was of his mate. They had heard the story before, probably from Jay, but they laughed boastfully and congratulated themselves for having such a fierce Lupa. It pleased Taye that they accepted her as a packmate. Carla was careful to look only at their faces, pretending their strong bare bodies didn't exist. Taye inwardly shook his head. She would get used to it eventually. Today was the last time he would wear clothes inside the den.

After breakfast he kissed his mate and said he was

going out to do a little training. He liked the way her face pinched with worry and her eyes went to the mostly healed gouge in his belly. "Yes, I'll be careful," he teased, kissing her again. He stripped off his cutoffs and handed them to her. "Put these in our room."

She was still gaping at him when he went outside and called his wolf.

———

Carla blinked at that very fine backside before it grew furry and turned into a wolf's behind. Good lord. She carefully folded the sweatpants before turning around and marching back to their room. She passed several men, all of whom called cheerful greetings to her. She nodded back.

Now what she supposed to do? Clean? The room was practically spotless. Laundry? Her clothes were as clean as a scrub in cold water in a bathtub could make them. She was going to spend the rest of her life here, doing what exactly? Being married to Taye wouldn't be too bad. He got a little bossy sometimes, but that probably went with being in charge. But what was she supposed to *do*? She was used to being busy. Becoming a country music star had been her goal for several years. She had worked hard for that career. Now what was she? A housewife? Not that she had anything against housewives. But she felt useless. What was she supposed to do? She could still write music in her head, but who would ever hear it? Sex with Taye wouldn't be a burden, but that wouldn't keep her busy during the day.

She sat down at the table and remembered this morning in bed with Taye. They had actually done very little, not even kissing. A little petting, that's all. But he'd had her all hot and bothered in about fifteen seconds. And they hadn't even kissed! She liked the last time he'd kissed her, and how his fingers had moved inside her...

She cut off that line of thought and got her notebook out to work on "Sleeping With the Wolf" and was soon buried in songwriting.

It was hours later that she heard voices calling, saying something about the Alpha's order to get dressed. Dressed? The wolves were going to put clothes on? Her tummy rumbled, and she glanced at her watch to see how long she had been in here. 11:30? Was the battery still working or had it died last night at 11:30? The door opened and Taye strolled in, naked.

"Sweetheart, where are my pants? We have company."

She pointed at the dresser without looking lower than his chin until he had pulled on his shorts. Then she let her eyes roam. "You're hurt!" she accused, reaching for the scratches scoring his brown skin from the base of his throat to the bottom of his breastbone.

"Nah," he said, scooping an arm around her shoulders. "Just a surface scratch. It'll heal up before supper. But if you'd like to kiss it better…"

She snorted.

He grinned. "That's what I thought. Come on to the rec room. We have visitors I want you to meet."

Carla went readily enough. She wondered how rare visitors were. They must not be the wolf kin from the tribe on the plains or clothing would not be required. It looked like the rec room was overflowing with bare-chested men wearing only shorts or pants. There was a happy party atmosphere in the room as the wolves laughed and talked together. Taye led her through them, and the men made an open path to the table by the large fireplace. Two men stood there, one tall and thin and very old, and the other tall and thin and young. Carla blinked because it seemed strange that they were fully dressed. The younger man looked familiar.

"Carla," Taye said. "This is Mr. Gray and his grandson, Doug Gray."

Carla froze for a minute, remembering Doug Gray from the Bride Fight. He had been one of the final four, and she remembered thinking he wouldn't be so bad as a husband. She smiled and reached to the older man to shake hands. Taye growled. The old man smiled and stepped back behind the table as Carla turned to Taye in surprise. Before she could ask what he thought he was doing, he pushed her behind him and growled again. Other wolves stepped up to flank Taye and block her in. The party atmosphere was gone, smothered by the threat of violence.

"Hey!" she said loudly.

She pushed the wolves aside, and she knew she could do it only because they let her. But she stepped up alongside Taye again and put her arm around his waist. He was vibrating with aggression. Good grief. She put her other arm around him, so she was hugging him and standing sideways to the visitors. She pretended that was normal and nodded politely to them.

"I'm very glad to meet you, Mr. Gray, and—" She hesitated very briefly, thinking Taye might not like it if she called the younger man by his first name. "—Mr. Gray."

"Likewise, Mrs. Wolfe," said the older man pleasantly, calmly, as if a wolf in human skin wasn't ready to tear out his throat. "Word came to us that your husband was looking for a trade item. If you'll excuse me…" He bent over to pull something out from under the table. The younger man also bent to help his grandfather.

Carla took that opportunity to pinch Taye. "Behave," she hissed.

"Do not *ever* touch another man," he hissed back.

She restrained herself from rolling her eyes. "Fine."

"You're mine."

"I know that." But they were going to have a talk. She scowled to let him know that.

Some of his aggression seeped away. The other wolves also relaxed. It wasn't quite back to the party mood, but the threat of violence was gone. Honestly, what did Taye think she was going to do? Run away from him to be the love slave of a man old enough to be her grandfather? It would—maybe—be more understandable if she had tried to shake the younger man's hand. He had tried to win her in the Bride Fight, and he would be considered very good-looking anywhere except in a room full of virile wolves.

Taye smoothed a hand over her hair. "You can let me go now," he whispered. "I've decided not to attack."

Carla wasn't sure if he were joking or not. She narrowed her eyes at him. "You better not," she said very quietly in his ear, "or I swear, you'll be sleeping on the couch."

A couple of the wolves coughed to cover laughter. She turned her head to glare at them, too. They ducked their heads to hide their grins. "What?" she snapped at them.

They all tilted their heads back to show their throats. She sighed and dropped one arm from Taye's waist.

The two visitors were moving slowly and deliberately as they lifted cases from the floor to put them on the table. Black, oddly shaped ... Guitar cases! Carla's heart bounded, suddenly longing profoundly for a guitar to play. She glanced up at Taye and he was smiling at her.

The older Mr. Gray opened the first case, and the younger Mr. Gray opened the second. "Both of these guitars are from the Times Before," said the elder, "and each is in good condition. Would you like to try them, Mrs. Wolfe, before choosing which you would like?"

"Me?" Carla gasped. She turned her head to look at Taye. "For me?"

"Of course, for you." The growl was gone from his voice, replaced by tenderness. "You miss your music." His broad shoulders rippled in an almost shrug. "I thought you would like it."

Carla hated crying in public. She tightened her arm around his waist. "I love it. Thank you."

His smile said that he heard all the grateful joy she'd tried to suppress. He nudged her forward. "Go ahead, try them out."

As she came forward the Grays stepped back. Carla

took over twenty minutes to play each of the guitars, tightening strings and plucking them to tune the instruments and then playing a song or two. She didn't see the pride brimming in Taye, or the fascination of the other wolves, or the faint look of nostalgia in the elder Mr. Gray.

When she finally selected the guitar she wanted, old Mr. Gray smiled. "That's a good choice. That guitar belonged to my wife."

"Oh," Carla drew back. "I can't take that one."

"I wish you would. None of my grandchildren have any interest in playing. That guitar should be played by someone who loves music. It came from Omaha with my wife. She loved your music. She would be glad to know you had it."

Carla's stomach fell to her feet. "Your wife ... You were alive then. In the Times Before, I mean."

"Yes. I was twenty-two years old when the world ended. I hiked west from Illinois and when I got to Omaha I met my Kylie. I worked for her father about a year. We married, and we came out here with our stuff loaded in a wheelbarrow. We took turns carrying that guitar for two hundred miles. She played it every night of that journey, singing love songs. I never was a country music fan until she started playing for me."

Carla held the guitar out. "I can't take this."

"It would have thrilled her to know you survived and that you had her guitar."

Carla stroked the frets. "Where is she?"

"Dead. She died over twenty years ago."

"I'm so sorry." Carla swallowed. "I would be honored to play her guitar."

Taye reached to catch the tear that slipped down her face with a callused forefinger. "What is your price?"

"I'd like to say it's a gift," the old man said, "but you wouldn't accept that, I suppose."

"Yes," said Carla firmly. "We will accept it as a gift. You can't put a price on precious memories. But we will give you a gift too. Tell me your wife's favorite songs, and I'll play them for you."

Taye opened his mouth, and Carla gave him a hard stare. Taye met it for a moment before bowing his head. "That is a good trade," he said almost meekly.

"I would like that very much," Mr. Gray said, with obvious gratitude. "My whole family would enjoy that. Could you come to us? With an escort, of course," he added to Taye. "The library is neutral territory, and we could fit the whole family there."

Taye thought about it. Carla gave him a look that was equal parts pleading and demanding. He nodded. "Next Sunday afternoon, after the midday meal."

"Done!" said the old man with delight. "Now,

anything you want to play would be just fine. Kylie was especially fond of the songs on your CD. She liked the old stuff too, like Dolly Parton and Emmy Lou Harris, and new stuff like Lady Antebellum and Miranda Lambert. Well, it was new in 2014. It will be a real lift to hear that music on that guitar again."

Carla nodded and hugged the guitar to keep from hugging him. Taye had gone wild over a handshake. A hug would probably make him homicidal. She had a gig! "I'll be looking forward to it."

Mr. Gray looked over at Taye. "With your permission, I'll invite Eddie and Lisa Madison to come too. I think Lisa would enjoy it."

Carla nodded enthusiastically. "Do you know Lisa? Have you met her? How is she?"

"I have. I met her yesterday at the library, and dropped by the Madison House this morning to see how she and Eddie were. They seem to be doing … well. When she heard I was coming here she asked me to say hello to you." He looked again at Taye for his consent.

Taye inclined his head. "The Madison family can come."

"That sounds real good. Mrs. Wolfe, there are a few extra strings here in this pocket. You might want to put the word out so the next trader to come through can have some for you."

Right. Carla doubted there were any music stores in this new world and no online stores to order from. "Thanks, I'll do that. Will you join us for lunch?"

The wolves went still, and Doug Gray dropped back another step. Carla knew she had done something wrong again. What? Invite a couple guys to stay for lunch? Was that worse than offering to shake hands with an old man?

"No, thank you," Mr. Gray said easily. "Me and Doug are headed out to Dane Overdahl's settlement. His brother Neal is taken with my granddaughter Ellie. She's my youngest daughter's only child. We're going to see if we can make a match for them."

"How nice," Carla said blankly. Matchmaking? Arranged marriages? What a screwed-up world. The remark had seemed to be pointed in Taye's direction, but why? Taye was already married.

Taye had stiffened slightly. "Ellie's father is Mart Burnett."

"That's right," said Mr. Gray, still pleasant. "Mart died three weeks ago. Ellie's moved into my place now, and she's my responsibility. She'll be glad to meet you on Sunday."

Carla was startled by Taye's hand on her waist squeezing tight and the bitterness in his voice. "Will she?"

It was Doug Gray who answered. "Ellie's not like her father. She pestered us to bring her today so she could meet you. Heck, she even thought about coming here to live after her father died, but … That was before Mrs. Wolfe came. A seventeen-year-old human girl with an all-male wolf pack … I don't think it would have been proper."

Taye's hand relaxed. "Probably not. I would have liked for you to bring her today."

Old Mr. Gray shook his head gently. "I would have liked to, but traveling with a young woman would have required a larger escort than just two men, especially when one is an old man like me. We couldn't take a crowd to Dane's, and besides, it's not appropriate to bring the bride-to-be to the marriage negotiations."

"Next time you could send me word, and I'll send some of the pack to guard her. She could stay here and visit my mate while you go on to Dane's." Carla thought Taye's voice was strange. Deep and rough and a bit uneven.

"Sounds like a plan," Mr. Gray agreed. "We'll do that next time."

"Good. You're welcome to stay for lunch."

"That's an honor. We appreciate the invitation, but we're hoping to make it to Dane's before supper. Maybe when we bring Ellie up this way we could join you?"

Taye nodded. "Anytime. It's an open invitation."

Carla watched and listened with a hundred thoughts and questions whirling through her mind. Taye walked the visitors out to the yard. The Grays nodded to her on the way out without offering to shake hands. She held her new guitar while the pack drifted around her, stripping off their pants and shorts and leaving them on the floor. She roused herself from her confusing thoughts to point accusingly.

"Are you just going to leave your clothes on the floor?" she demanded. "How will you tell whose is whose?"

They looked at her and shrugged. It was the teenager, Sky, who said, "Who cares? What fits one of us will fit the others just as well. We just share them."

Well, yes, Carla realized, they all had the same lean, muscular build. Still. "Well, don't leave them out here. Go put them away."

"Yes, Lupa."

Amazing. Werewolves obeyed her.

Taye came in and wrapped his arms gently around her. "Sweetheart," he said into her hair. His voice was shaky.

"You okay?"

"Yes." He lifted his head and tucked a lock of hair

behind her ear. "Just … happy. I have a beautiful mate who is pleased with my gift. And I have a cousin who wants to know me."

"That's great. I love the guitar. Thank you so much for thinking of it." Carla peeked around and saw some of the other wolves watching them and decided against kissing Taye. She put her arms around his waist and squeezed gently instead. "I guess you haven't met Ellie? Don't you have other cousins?"

"Many, with the Clan on the plains. My father had three brothers and they all had sons. No daughters. But it's different with my mother's kin. Let's go to our room, and I'll tell you of my mother and father."

He sounded serious and sad. Carla put the guitar in its case and left it on the table. Taye sounded like this would be a serious conversation. She walked with him down the hall with one arm around his waist. In their room Carla sat on the couch and Taye sprawled on the cushions with his head in her lap. He held her hand and rubbed it against his cheek.

"My mother was the daughter of a human. Her name was Naomi Burnett. She grew up in Odessa, the same farming settlement you found just southwest of town. My father was hunting with friends when they came to Odessa. My mother was working in the fields and as soon as he saw her, his wolf chose her to be his mate. He went to talk to her, but she was scared when he turned from wolf to human in front of her. She tried to run away. It's not good to run away from a wolf, especially a young one without enough experience to have learned self control. Carla, never run away from a wolf. Promise me."

A feeling of dread trickled over her. "Okay. So what happened? Did your dad hurt her?"

Taye was rubbing the back of her hand back and forth over his lips. "He chased her. Wolves run fast even when they're human. When he caught her he threw her down and marked her. He bit her here." His fingers brushed over the place where her neck joined her shoulder. "Hard enough to draw blood. Wolves sometimes do that when they are agitated and unsure of their mate's acceptance. He had been hunting in his fur, and when he changed to human to talk to her he was naked. My mother was terrified. She thought he would hurt her." He fell silent, a troubled frown on his face. "No wolf would intentionally hurt his mate, but my father was young, only sixteen—"

"Sixteen?" gasped Carla.

"—and my mother was fighting."

"Oh, God, he raped her?"

"No. He might have, but when he saw that she was crying and smelled her fear, he let her go. She ran back to her settlement and he didn't stop her. Instead, he thought he would try to court her the human way. Do you understand about wolves choosing a mate? Human men can marry where they like or where their families decide, but wolves don't have that choice. Our wolves choose a mate for us. Some men give up on waiting for their wolves to choose a mate. They just marry a woman the human way. But a wife's not fully accepted by the Pack the way mate is. Once a mate has been chosen, we can never have another woman."

"Your wolf chose me. I remember you saying that. But how did you know?"

His shoulders moved in a shrug. "I just did. My father knew the same way. It's like the wolf whispers in our hearts, 'That's the one I want.' He went back a few days later, wearing his best clothes, with a string of horses to give her family for her bride price. Her brother, Mart Burnett, tried to kill him before he was even inside the gates. So my father ran away. He came back later with friends and watched the settlement for days for his chance to take his mate. My mother and some other girls and men came out to work in the fields again, and my father's friends attacked them. He stole my mother and took her to the Clan."

"Your poor mother," Carla said. The Bride Fight didn't seem quite so scary compared to that. Since Taye had been born his parents had obviously been intimate. Had it been rape? Had his mother submitted passively to his father out of fear? Or had she fallen in love with her kidnapper? "How old was she?"

"A little older. About nineteen, I think. She had been promised to a neighbor, and she had loved him until he rejected her for being pawed by a 'filthy wolf.'" Taye smiled a crooked smile. "My father spent three years courting her while she lived with the Clan's grandmother. He was successful. I remember how much they loved each other. But she missed her human family. About a year after I was born they went to her family to try to reconcile. Her family wouldn't even see them. It broke my mother's heart, and anything that hurt her hurt my father."

Carla combed her fingers through his soft short hair. "Where are your parents now?"

"They're both dead. My father died when I was fourteen. My mother wanted to be with humans so she brought me here. Some of the clan came with us, because they didn't want us to be alone. She worked hard to make this place a good home. The rugs and the quilts are some of the things she made for me. She went to Odessa every year on her birthday to beg her brother to accept us back into her family, but he was cruel. I think he liked hurting her. She died three years ago, and she made me promise to never harm her family." His voice sank to a growl. "Otherwise he would have died sooner."

"Oh, how awful for your mother. How could her brother have done that? What an evil man."

"He said I was vermin."

"What?" said Carla, outraged.

"Because I'm a wolf. Some humans feel that way about us. I'm glad you don't."

Carla didn't know exactly how she felt about it. The whole wolf thing seemed unbelievable, but every time she saw him change she was reminded that it was real. "Tell me about the Clan."

"When the world ended, some of the ancestors who lived on the reservation decided to leave and live on the prairie in the old way. They were members of the Wolf Clan and their friends. My grandfather and his brothers were among them. Our Pack is actually part of the Clan, but we live separate from them. I'll take you to the Clan soon, and you can hear my uncle tell our history."

"Should you do that? I'm not a wolf."

"You're a member of the Pack. And you didn't reject me or my wolf. I worried about it the whole time we were walking home from the Bride Fight," Taye confessed. "I didn't know if you would scream when

124

you saw my wolf or try to run away … I didn't expect you to pet me. But I'm glad you did. Feel free to pet me anytime."

So Carla did, stroking his hair and letting her hand sweep lightly over his arm.

"Just don't bite me," she warned.

"Maybe just a little nip?" he teased.

"Hmmm," she said dubiously.

Taye kissed the back of her hand. "I knew I had a girl cousin but I never saw her. When my mother and I went to Odessa all the settlement's women were hidden away. I have about twenty cousins in the Clan, but they are all boys. Girls are rare, and I always wanted to have a sister to protect and spoil, but I thought Ellie felt the same way as her father."

"Well, she doesn't. And you'll get to meet her in a few days. It'll be nice for you. Do you know Neal? The guy she might be marrying?"

"I've met him, but I don't know him." He frowned. "I should get to know him. Just to be sure he treats her right. If he hurts her in any way I'll kill him."

Carla believed him. Another man might say that and he'd be blowing off steam or exaggerating. Taye was calmly serious. She poked him in the shoulder with a disapproving finger. "Taye, we have to work on your aggression. You can't go around killing people. Or growling at them, either."

"I can if they threaten me or someone I care about."

"Mr. Gray? How was he threatening you?"

"You were going to touch him."

"That's what people do when they meet. They shake hands."

"Never touch any man who's not Pack or Clan. My wolf won't allow it."

Carla rolled her eyes. "Paranoid, much?"

Taye lifted his head off her lap and half sat up. "Carla, this is important. You get too friendly with a strange man, and I'll likely kill him. My wolf is very possessive of you."

"Honestly! Could you be a little more bossy? Don't you think killing someone for shaking hands is a teeny little bit much? It's called overkill, Taye."

"I'm an Alpha. Mostly, I can control myself, but you bring my wolf out. In this one thing you have to follow the rules."

"Taye, I don't understand about you and your wolf. You talk like … Are you separate from your wolf? Or are you one person? When you turn into the wolf are you still Taye? And when you're human—" She broke off when her stomach growled and Taye leapt to his feet.

"We're missing lunch! You missed lunch yesterday,

too, and you're already too skinny. Come on. I'll tell you all about wolves while we eat."

The dining room was almost empty when they got there. Lunch was steak with fried potatoes. Carla took her steak into the kitchen and put it back on the grill to finish cooking. She decided she would have to do something about the menu around here. It would be something to do. Although, now that she had a guitar, maybe she could do concerts. She carried her steak back to the table and waited for Taye to illuminate her about the secret lives of werewolves.

The first thing she learned was that they weren't born as puppies, so she would have regular human babies. Carla hadn't even thought that she would give birth at all, much less to a wolf pup. Even if she and Taye had sex—and looking across the table at him, she had no doubt that they would—it would be a year before she could become pregnant thanks to her contraceptive shot. The children of the Pack were born human and sometime soon after puberty the wolf would force a change. If a boy got to be fifteen without making the change, then he was a full member of the Pack, but not wolf-born. He was still faster and stronger than a human, and healed more quickly, and could have sons who would be wolves. Carla asked about girls, and Taye told her that no girl was ever a wolf.

"That sucks!" Carla protested. "Why not?"

"They're girls," Taye said dismissively, as if that explained it.

Taye and his wolf were two beings who shared his body. When he was a man the wolf was pushed into a quiet cage in his mind unless he was agitated for some reason. But Taye the man was dominant over the wolf, so the wolf couldn't break out of the cage without severe provocation. Some wolves, especially when the human was very young, or less dominant, could take control. It took time to learn to manage the wolf. When Taye was a wolf he was the one who was pushed aside. The wolf's wants and desires were simple: food to eat, the joy of hunting, a Pack to be part of, a mate to cherish and protect.

Carla shifted uneasily, horrified by her thoughts. "Taye," she whispered. "When we … you know. You're not going to be a wolf, right? Ever. Because, that is *not* going to happen."

"You mean sex?" Taye said calmly. "My wolf doesn't want you sexually. He leaves that part to me."

"Oh, good. I was scared there for a minute. But I thought he was the one who picked me?"

"He did. To be his special companion. He wants you to be the person who belongs to him, kind of like … a horse belongs to a human."

Carla stared at him blankly. "A horse?"

Taye frown and shook his head. "That's not a good description. It's like…"

As Taye trailed off, obviously frustrated to not be able to explain better, another man stepped up to the table. He had light brown hair in a tangled mess hanging in his face and past his shoulders and vivid green eyes peering through it. "I heard my father explain it once to my mother. He said that to his wolf, she was like the only warm house in the middle of a deadly blizzard. She gave him a safe place to shelter in, one that was just for him, and he would take care of that safe place and defend it from intruders."

Carla's mouth formed an "Oh," without sound. Then, "Is that why the wolf doesn't want me to shake hands with other men? He thinks that might let them into his safe shelter?"

"Exactly," said Taye with relief. He rested a hand on the other man's arm. "Thanks, Quill."

Quill had a shy smile of surpassing sweetness, and Carla reduced her estimate of his age from early twenties to late teens. As he walked away, Carla realized she had looked at him without embarrassment because she hadn't even noticed he wasn't wearing clothes. Maybe she was getting used to it.

Taye took her hand and pressed it against his cheek.

"So you see why you need to stay away from strange men? Will you do that for me?"

"I guess."

Taye got up and kissed her gently on the lips. "I'm going out to train again this afternoon. You can play with your gift. I'll see you at supper."

The scratches across his chest were faint, almost completely healed. Carla touched them lightly. "I haven't really thanked you yet for the guitar. It's the best present I've ever gotten."

Taye's smile was wicked. "You can thank me tonight. After supper. When we've retired to our room."

Carla's blush was hot. "O-o-okay," she stuttered, remembering the way his fingers worked her last night.

After he stripped off his sweatpants and handed them to her to put away, she took one long deliberate look at him. And she liked what she saw. He didn't seem to notice, only smiling at her and leaving the dining room. Carla fanned her face for a minute, then gathered their dishes to take into the kitchen.

The kitchen was in the process of lunch clean up. Three teenagers were there washing dishes, cleaning the grill, and wiping the counters. Sky was one. He nodded to her and took her tray. He sniffed delicately at her.

"So, you and the Chief finally gonna do it tonight?"

Carla opened her mouth to snap that it was none of

his business. But Taye had explained that the Pack was family, and they all cared deeply for each other. The human concept of privacy didn't exist in Pack life. As Lupa she was like their mother.

"We'll see," she finally muttered.

"I bet you will," he predicted cheerfully. "You smell like you really like him."

Carla escaped from the kitchen and headed to her guitar in the rec room. There were a few men lounging there, and when they saw she was opening the guitar case they begged her to play for them. So she did. It wasn't long before she had a dozen listeners. But most of the songs she was singing had lyrics that talked about things they couldn't comprehend, like divorce and cheating, or phones and trucks, so she switched to other, lighter songs. The dozen men swelled to an audience of about twenty-five. She sang a song she had written a few months ago but never recorded about a young girl who loved rainstorms and then one about a mother's love for her soldier son. The audience was responsive. Who would have thought that a song about a man who loved a girl who married someone else would bring werewolves to tears? They leaned against one another, a pile of naked muscular men weeping for a made-up lover in a song. She lightened the mood by singing a silly children's song. Carla loved the sound of this guitar and felt a wave of gratitude for Taye's generosity. And a wave of sadness for old Mr. Gray's loss of his wife. She should write a song for him about this old guitar and the journey it had taken, carried by a man who loved the woman who had played it. She launched into the upbeat chorus of "Sleeping With the Wolf," but without the words. She needed to finish that song, but she was waiting for current events to unfold to know how the song would end.

When she finished she looked up and saw that the rec room was filled with silent wolves, including Taye. She laid the guitar carefully aside and went to him, and kissed his lips softly.

"I love my guitar, Taye. Thank you from the bottom of my heart."

He returned the kiss just as gently. "You're welcome, mate. I love you and I want you to be happy."

How was a woman to keep from falling in love with a man like this?

Taye saw his pants folded on the table and went to put them on. Carla watched, enjoying the way the muscles in his back, butt, and thighs stretched and bunched as he moved. He didn't have the bulky physique of a body builder, with muscles bulging and veins popping, but the leaner build of a swimmer. Each muscle was hard and defined, and he moved with the smooth feral grace that all the wolves had. What would he be like in bed? He saw her staring and lifted an inquiring eyebrow. Carla pretended she had been examining him for injuries.

"You didn't get hurt again, did you?"

He smiled and held his arms out, inviting her to see for herself. "Not even a scratch. I am perfectly well."

She stepped closer, looking critically at the red mark below his belly button which was all that was left from his fight with Pete. Her finger barely grazed the top edge, and his belly muscles jumped. "How about this?"

"That is healed," he said huskily. "I am completely whole, sweetheart. May I seduce you tonight?"

Carla's tummy fluttered with nerves and maybe anticipation. "Does a man have to seduce his own wife?"

"I don't know. I've never had one before." His mouth smiled, but his eyes were serious. "I'd say that is up to you."

The nerves grew, but after a moment, anticipation covered it. "I'd say I might like being seduced tonight."

Now his eyes smiled too, and he looked like a kid who had just unwrapped the one Christmas present he had most hoped for. "Then I will seduce you. I have it all planned out, step-by-step."

"You've planned it? How many steps did you plan?"

He winked at her. "You'll find out."

He put his arm around her shoulders and pulled her along with him toward the hallway. She dug her heels in. "Not right this second!"

His surprise melted into a chuckle. "No, I'm going to take a shower before supper."

"Oh." Relief made her heart pound. "Okay."

He sniffed at her. "Are you scared?"

"No." When the worry on his face didn't go away, she added, "Just a little nervous."

"Oh. I guess it's up to me to calm your nerves. It's in the plan."

"Well, then. I'll just leave that all up to you. Go ahead and take your shower. I'll hang out here with my guitar."

She went back to her guitar and held it like a baby for comfort. Not that she was really frightened. She was actually looking forward to being with Taye. This was just wedding night jitters. Some of the wolves saw her with her guitar and clustered around her.

"No, I'm not going to play right now," she told them.

"Maybe after supper?" the one who looked fourteen said hopefully.

Sky answered for her. "Can't you smell her, Jelly?

134

She's gonna be busy tonight."

Carla blushed, and the kid looked mystified.

"She'll be busy with the Chief," Sky clarified impatiently.

"Oh," said the kid, with an adult's comprehension. "That'll make the Chief happy."

Carla put her forehead in her palm and shook her head. Everybody knew what she and Taye were going to do, even the kids. This was so embarrassing.

"What's wrong, Lupa?" the kid asked. He petted her arm anxiously. "Are you hurt?"

"No," Carla mumbled. "I'll play a few songs tonight after supper, okay? Just leave me alone for now."

She was getting used to Taye's smell. It was hot and masculine. She knew he was standing beside her and looked up at him awkwardly. His hair was still damp from his shower, finger combed, from the spiky look of it. Carla thought he had never looked better. "That was a quick shower."

He smiled, and it made him look boyish. "It doesn't take me long. I don't have hair down to my waist, like some wolves do. So you're going to sing for us tonight?"

"Just a few songs. If you don't mind."

"I don't mind. That will fit with my plans just fine."

Carla stroked a hand over his arm. "I was thinking. Everyone seems to like my music. I'm really looking

135

forward to playing on Sunday. I'd like to do that for other people too. You know, do some concerts like I did back ho—I mean, in the Times Before."

Taye didn't even stop to think about it. "No."

Carla took a step back. His autocratic tone made her bristle. "No? That's it?"

"My mate doesn't expose herself to strange men."

"What? Taye, this is what I do. This is who I am. I have to have something to do."

Taye looked down at her with stern eyes. "You're my mate. The den is your responsibility. And we'll have children soon."

Carla folded her arms over her chest. "Even if we have sex morning, noon, and night there will be no babies for a while. I had my contraceptive shot a week before I got on the plane."

The look of revulsion in his eyes hurt her. "In the Times Before people tried to prevent babies? I had heard of it, and read about it in books. But I can't believe it. Why would you do that?"

"Because … Never mind that now. My music is important to me. I need to perform. Not national tours. I get that. But maybe in some of the nearby towns and settlements."

"It's too dangerous to let you go to strange places."

"It wouldn't have to be strange places, and I would

never go by myself," Carla argued. She could see that she wasn't budging him. "You remember the sex you wanted to have tonight?"

"Carla." He sighed. "You promised me you would stay away from other men."

"I will." The type of concerts she was imagining were nothing like the concerts she had given in the past. She wouldn't be wearing short skirts or pulling a guy from the audience to dance with. She let her arms drop. "Taye, my music is as important to me as being a wolf is to you. Don't take that away from me."

He curled a hand over her wrist. "Would you really refuse me sex?"

Carla blew out air. "No."

His hand began smoothing up and down her arm. "I'll think about it. Maybe when my wolf has settled we can arrange something for you."

It was better than the flat-out refusal he had first given her. She slid an arm around his waist. "Let's go eat."

CHAPTER SEVEN

They ate supper sitting side by side at the head table facing the pack, and while they ate Carla wondered about those steps of his that he had planned out. He spent quite a bit of the time laughing with the other pack members and telling stories about some hunt he had been on last year. Since he wasn't focusing on her she was able to relax. Supper was—surprise, surprise!—steak. She really would have to introduce them to some other foods. She didn't expect wolves to be vegetarians, but there were ways to prepare meat besides grilling slabs of it until it was just barely warm. She thought Taye was ignoring her, but every now and then his large, warm hand would settle on her thigh and rub circles over the denim of her jeans, and she would jerk in an unsteady breath. How long before they could go to their room?

The three teenagers who apparently had kitchen duty all day hurried the diners so they could get the kitchen cleaned up before Carla began playing. It was flattering to have such an eager audience. While she waited for her audience to gather, she mentally ran through all the songs she knew about wolves, which were very few. Werewolves of London was about it, and she didn't even know all the lyrics. Right about now the internet would come in handy.

Taye sat beside her near the fireplace in the rec room and held the end of her braid in his hand while she strummed and decided on a few songs. Instead of wolf songs, she would sing love songs. With her audience hanging on the words, she sang "I Swear" and "It's Your Love," and finished with "Love Me Tender." Then she put the guitar away and whispered to Taye to give her fifteen or twenty minutes by herself in their room before he came.

The wolves all howled raucously when she left, and she waved at them. They didn't clap so this must be their version of applause. Carla wasn't sure what they were applauding, her music or her wedding night. In their room the lamps were lit, but the wicks were low so the light was only a soft golden glow. The stove was putting out a comforting warmth. The sheets on the bed must have been changed, because the edge that was folded over the top of the quilt was embroidered with red poppies. Taye must have prepared the room for them. For tonight. He was a werewolf who had killed a vicious opponent only a few days ago, but to her he was very sweet. And utterly gorgeous. She hurried to the bathroom and washed and brushed her teeth. She dithered over getting undressed and putting on Taye's T-shirt, but in the end decided not to. Then she dithered over taking her braid out and leaving her hair down. And that was when Taye came in. She turned to face him, clutching the comb like a weapon. He was magnificent in only a pair of cut-off sweatpants that rode low on his hips. The muscles of his bare chest gleamed in the lamplight. She was definitely overdressed.

"Now you're frightened," he said sadly.

"No, just a little nervous," she insisted. "Do you want me to ... uh, get undressed?"

"No, that comes later in the plan. Come here, sweetheart. Let me just hold you."

She went to him and put her arms around his waist, still holding the comb. His bare shoulder was warm against her cheek, and his scent aroused her. "Is this Step One?"

"Step One is to make sure you are not frightened." He ran his hands up and down her spine. "Step Two is to make sure you are relaxed."

"Got any beer?" she asked, half joking.

"No, no beer. Here, sit down and give me the comb. I'll comb your hair for you."

Carla sat on the couch, half facing away from him behind her. She had never had anyone comb her hair except the beautician. She gave him the comb and felt his fingers loosening her braid. He was amazingly gentle when he separated the strands that had knotted at the nape of her neck. After carefully working out the few tangles, the comb slid through her hair in long lazy sweeps. It felt amazing.

"I've wanted to touch your hair like this since the night I saw you at Ray's," Taye murmured.

"Well," she sighed. "You can comb my hair anytime. That feels so nice."

The comb continued to glide through her hair, followed by a caressing hand. His fingers moved under her hair to smooth over her neck and shoulder under her blouse. After a minute he swept her hair to one side to press a kiss to her nape. A row of featherlight kisses went from behind her ear, down the side of her neck, to her collarbone. She turned on the seat so she could see him. His cheeks were slightly flushed, and she lifted a hand to test the heat of his face. He caught it before she could touch him.

"It's not time for that step yet."

"What step?" Carla blinked.

"You don't get to touch me until after I've satisfied you." He lowered her hand to her knee. "I've studied those romance books from the Times Before, and in every one of them the lady was pleasured first. Then the man. Now hush so I can continue with my plan."

Carla had to work to suppress her chuckle. She found her hand moving subtly on her knee, wishing it were his hand. "You know, Taye, those are only stories. In real life it doesn't work like that."

"Hush," he said sternly. "It's my plan. Your job is to relax and enjoy."

"Relax and enjoy. I can handle that. I think. What's the next step?"

"Next—" His finger slipped inside her blouse and ran under the top edge of her bra over one breast. "—I get to see what your pantie look like when they are on you."

Her hands went obediently to the top button on her blouse.

"No," he growled. "I get to do that."

He waited until she replaced her hands in her lap

and then unbuttoned each button with slow, deliberate fingers. Those fingers trembled ever so slightly when they brushed the tops of her breasts above the pink satin bra while spreading her blouse wide. Carla shuddered a little from the cool air and his eyes on her hot, exposed skin. "Are you cold?" he whispered.

"With you looking at me like that? I wouldn't be cold if we were sitting outside in January."

"I like looking at you. Are you as soft as you look?"

Carla had to force herself to not squirm. "I guess you'll have to touch to find out."

The feel of his fingers trailing down along the shoulder strap of her bra and curling to brush his knuckles over the curve of her breast made excitement flood through her. He brushed his knuckles back and forth over her puckered nipple until she was quivering.

"Taye, that's my bra. You can't tell if I'm soft by touching that."

He hooked a thumb under the shoulder strap beside her armpit. "How does it come off?"

"There's a fastener right in the front." Carla was surprised how hoarse her voice was. "See that round button there? Just—"

Her bra opened, and Taye pulled the front edges apart, releasing her breasts. His eyes seemed to hold awe as he studied her curves and nipples. He pulled the edge of her pink bra back to one of her nipples. "It's almost the same color," he remarked, and she was glad that his voice sounded a little hoarse too.

"I'm sort of small," she apologized.

"Too thin," he agreed, stroking both hands over her ribs and rubbing her breasts with his thumbs. "No more missed lunches for you, sweetheart."

"No, I mean ... Never mind."

She loved the feel of his face rubbing over her chest. He would drag one cheek over her chest, then turn his head and drag the other over her, taking deep breaths all the while. "You smell like love, sweetheart."

He smelled fantastic too. His mouth opened and passed over her breast, and on the return pass he paused to taste her nipple with just his tongue. She shook and that seemed to encourage him to suck and nibble at her breast. She pressed her thighs together as heat shot through her. His teeth scraped over her taut nipple, and she grabbed his shoulders to keep from falling when a lightning bolt of sensation zinged through her.

He abandoned her breast to take her hands from his shoulders and put them back in her lap. "It's not time for that step yet, sweetheart."

"Taye! I have to hold onto something or I'll fall over!"

"Nope. Let me..." He slid her blouse and bra down

her arms and tossed them aside before lowering her so she was lying on the couch and he was kneeling on the floor beside her. Then he went back to feasting on her breasts.

"Taye," she complained breathlessly. "Can't we move along a little? You're torturing me."

"Step by step," he murmured to her nipple.

His mouth on her skin was like being thrown into a volcano. Carla gasped and lifted one knee to ease an ache that made her want to drag him down on top of her.

"Taye, lay on top of me."

He was breathing fast against her neck. "No, we're definitely not at that step yet. We're still in one of the foreplay steps."

"*One* of the foreplay steps? Taye, *please*."

"Uh-uh."

When his mouth returned to hers his hand rubbed up and down the inside seam of her jeans along her bent leg from calf to knee and slipped to the inside of her thigh. She squirmed to force his hand where she wanted it, and he let her. His hand opened and cupped her between her legs, and even through her jeans it felt good.

"Taye," she groaned. "Take my jeans off."

"I suppose we can skip a few steps," he said with

reluctance warring with eagerness in his eyes.

Carla barely managed to choke back a giggle. There had been a time she had expected him to tear her clothes off and get right to the main event. Never in a million years had she expected her wolf to drag it out like this. He pulled her boots and her socks off, and she wiggled her toes playfully. She quit wiggling, though, when his big hands hooked into the waistband of her jeans and dragged them slowly down. She lifted her hips to help him and soon they were gone, leaving her pink panties halfway down her thighs. Long moments passed with no sound from Taye, and no touch either. She lifted her head to see what he was doing. He was staring hard at her private place. She wondered why she didn't feel shy. Maybe because he was looking so reverent. She lifted her hips and wiggled to move the panties further down so she could kick them off. She didn't see where they landed, and he wasn't even watching. He caught her legs with a hand under each knee and opened her up to study her more thoroughly. Now she felt shy.

"Taye?"

"Hush. Let me look at you. This is so beautiful. I've never seen a woman's … What did they call it in those books? Pussy?"

Carla choked. "What kind of books have you been reading? Never mind," she said hastily. "Quit staring at me and let me go. Kiss me some more."

He held her legs further apart and pulled her closer to kiss her, but not on her mouth. His teeth grazed her and closed gently over an ultra-sensitive place. "Oh, my God! What are you doing?"

"Getting to know you," he answered innocently, but a devilish gleam lit his dark eyes. "See, I've read about this, but I've never seen one or touched one, so I need to familiarize myself with this marvelous body. Here—" He flicked a forefinger back and forth over her. "—is your clit. Your tender pearl of delight. This is supposed to feel good to a woman. Does it feel good?"

Carla's half-choked giggle turned into a groan. "Oh, yeah."

"I'll come back to that in a minute. First I want to explore a little more." She felt his fingers part her and cool air touch hot flesh that usually didn't get exposed to air. "And this is your labia. Or is that plural? These are your labia? They are like the castle walls guarding your prize. They are on the outside, but here, between them, is your vagina. One book I read called it the woman's hot tunnel of joy. I didn't understand that, but—" One of his fingers slid into her slowly. "—it is like a tunnel, isn't it? And you are warm inside."

Intense pleasure overwhelmed the amusement she had felt at the ridiculous descriptions of her body parts.

147

Her head fell back. "Taye, I love the way you touch me. But let's save some of that for later, okay? Take off your pants and—"

"No, no, sweetheart. It's not time for me to let my warrior of love conquer your tunnel yet."

"Your *what*?"

"My penis. He will have to wait a while yet. We're not ready for that step yet."

"No! I mean, yes, we are!"

"Your tunnel is wet, sweetheart. Slick. Is it always like this?"

Carla lifted her head to see his face peering at her with wonder. "No. I get like that only when you're kissing me or touching me." *Or when you're looking at me, or standing next to me, or when I think about you,* Carla said to herself.

Taye pressed a gentle kiss to the inside of her thigh. "You are precious, a better mate than I had even hoped for."

"Taye, quit dragging this out. I want you now!"

But Taye paid no attention to her protest. His teeth and tongue and fingers were busy with her castle walls and pearl of delight and exploring her tunnel. She clenched her teeth against a moan and tried to not writhe against him. "Stop torturing me, Taye! Please!"

He lifted his head, and his eyes were unfocused. "I

148

think we'll skip a few more steps tonight," he muttered in a rough voice.

"Thank God," she began to say, but he picked her up and carried her to the bed with long strides.

His plan with the multiple painstaking steps seemed to dissolve as soon as he pushed down his sweatpants and flung himself into the bed with her. His hand took hold of one of her thighs to open her wide while the other held her hands together over her head. His cock pushed against her opening, parting her in the most delicious way as he slid forcefully in. It had been so long since she had been with a guy. Was that why Taye felt so wonderful? Or was it just Taye? She didn't know and she didn't care.

Someone was panting hoarsely, almost growling, and she wasn't sure which of them it was. Opening her eyes to look up at him, she saw his face clenched and his teeth bared. He didn't look nearly as in control as he had earlier when he had been going from one step of his seduction to the next. His dark brown eyes glowed almost wolf-golden, sightless when he growled and panted and bit the pillow beside her head. He sawed back and forth inside her, sliding easily in their juices. Each time he pushed so deeply within her she felt her tremors intensify. Her orgasm seemed to explode inside her like a nuclear bomb. He continued to move forcefully inside her while she shook and trembled like a leaf dancing in the wind until he reared up on his knees and let out a howl that could have woke the dead. Held by thigh and wrists, she came up with him, almost howling herself. He let her go, and flopped down beside her, panting. She was panting herself, body still humming with climax.

"Sweetheart, did he hurt you?" Taye was up on one elbow again, running his hand frantically over her throat and shoulders. "Did he mark you?"

"Who?"

"My wolf. I lost control." He sounded like he was confessing to mass murder. "Are you okay?"

"I'm fine. I'm *really* fine." Carla tried to smother a giggle, but it burst out. "That was wonderful, Taye."

"He didn't bite you? I felt him biting."

Carla reached up and laid her hand on his cheek. So it *had* been the wolf she'd seen watching her. Should that repulse her? She wanted to brush away the guilt and worry she heard in his voice. "No, Taye, you didn't hurt me. You—he bit the pillow. Don't you know?"

He hid his face against her shoulder. "My wolf broke out. That hasn't happened since I was a boy. I couldn't stop him. He could have mauled you!"

Carla put her arm tight around his back. "Taye, he didn't hurt me at all. When your father—your father's wolf bit your mother she was running away, right? I wasn't running away. In fact, I was doing my best to get as close to you as I possibly could. Didn't you say that a wolf wouldn't hurt his mate?"

"Normally, no. But he was so strong tonight…"

She put her fingers through the sweat damp hair at his nape. "Did you know what was happening? It was your body, right?"

He lifted his head from her shoulder and lifted up on his elbow to meet her eyes with shame in his own. "I knew what was happening, but I wasn't in charge of it. I wanted our first time to be perfect. My plan for our wedding night didn't go the way I wanted it to. I wanted you to find pleasure before I did."

"Taye, I went before you did, believe me. Any more pleasure than that and I might have had a heart attack. You came after me." She searched his dark eyes. "Are you okay? Didn't you feel anything?"

"I felt everything." Remembered pleasure warmed his eyes. "It was…"

"Wow," she supplied.

"Wow," he agreed. He lay down beside her and lifted her head to his shoulder. "But I want to be in control next time we make love. I don't know if my wolf will let me, though. What if next time he breaks out again?"

Carla stroked his chest. "Then I'll tell him to go back because I want to be with you this time. Unless you plan to torture me again by dragging things out forever."

"It's fun to watch you squirm." He sounded innocent.

"Maybe I should be the one to torture you," she threatened. "You never even let me touch you tonight."

Taye's voice went from teasing to serious. "I'm Alpha. I have to be in control. I don't know how to not be."

"Taye…" Carla sighed. "That's not fair. Marriage is a two-way street. I can see how you'd need to be in control in other areas. But here in our bedroom? We're private. It's just us. I won't tell anyone if you let me be on top once in a while."

Taye thought about it. "The time after this next one you can be in charge," he offered generously.

"Oh, good. That will give me some time to plan my One Hundred Steps To Torture Taye With."

———

They teased back and forth for a while longer, until Carla dropped off to sleep. Taye continued to hold her, deeply thankful that his wolf hadn't harmed her. In his mind he sought out his wolf. They couldn't really speak to each other, but they communicated with feelings and some mental images. Taye made it clear to his wolf that Carla was precious, and when it came lovemaking, he, the human partner, would be in charge. The wolf made it clear that Taye had been hurting their mate by making her wait for his body, so he had taken over. Taye wondered if the wolf was right. Carla had protested more than once. She had wanted to touch him. He didn't want to lose control. Maybe she was right. In private he could pretend to submit to her. He told the wolf that from now on he would let Carla take control of their lovemaking at least some of the time, and he should butt out.

With that issue resolved, Taye curled up around Carla's wonderfully bare body and went to sleep.

Chapter Eight

There was daylight coming through the curtains when Carla woke, and it took her a minute to remember what had happened last night. She reached for Taye, but the bed was empty, and she didn't hear him in the bathroom. She stretched, curling her toes against the mattress. What a night! Taye was a forceful lover. She was going to have to teach him that lovemaking didn't have to be a fight for dominance. It was give and take equally. She had as much right to touch him and make him tremble as he did to touch her. It was a shame he was gone. She'd like to start the lessons now.

The air outside the cozy bedclothes was warm. Taye must have put wood in the stove before he left. Just a few days ago she had been terrified by the idea of being his mate. But everything he did was for her comfort. He showed how much he cared not by saying it but by doing it. Maybe it wasn't true love. Her mother had told her once years ago that love was a verb, not just a noun. She said true love was built over years of standing together and working together even when things were hard. She and Taye had known each other only a few days. But what they had could grow into true love. She was sure of it.

Carla folded back the covers and got up, stretching. One thing she was going to need pretty soon was a robe. All she had was Taye's T-shirt. She saw a note on the table and went to pick it up. The paper was thick, probably homemade. The writing was carefully formed. She wondered, as she unfolded the paper how much time a werewolf spent reading and writing. Had Taye gone to school? There was still so much she didn't know about him. She read the note.

Sweetheart, I have gone hunting. I'll be back before supper. There is hot water for a bath. Love, Taye.

Hot water! A week ago she hadn't valued hot water the way she should have. She went into the bathroom and luxuriated in a hot shower. Then she combed her wet hair and braided it and put on her same clothes. The blood stains hadn't come out. Shopping was going to be a priority. She would talk to Taye about it when he got home. Meanwhile, she would eat, then work on her music for the concert on Sunday.

The den was almost deserted. Apparently most of the wolves were gone hunting. There were two men in the rec room, and she was pretty sure they were human, not wolf born. How she knew that she wasn't sure. One was blond and the other had light brown hair, but both were wearing the wolves' usual dress of nothing at all. She nodded at them as she went into the kitchen and scooped herself some lukewarm oatmeal and grabbed an apple. She ate the oatmeal quickly and took the apple and her guitar back to her room.

As always, Carla lost herself in her music. She was able to write the song for Mr. Gray. It talked about sweet Kylie and the young Mr. Gray who loved her. She used the guitar as a symbol of their love, how they took turns carrying it on their journey to a new home and how its songs had strengthened them on the long weary evenings of the journey. With only the guitar for an instrument it was a simple sweet melody. It was, Carla thought, possibly the best song she had ever written, and she wished she could record it. She thought only an hour had passed, but when she came back to herself she found the sun was low, and noises in the hallway indicated that the wolves were back from hunting. And she was starving.

She laid aside her guitar and went out to see about supper and if Taye was back yet. He was right outside their door, holding a large cloth-wrapped parcel. It was almost as large as she was. He dropped it on the floor and leaned into her. His weight rested solidly against her chest and pushed her back into the closed door of their room. He smiled into her eyes and kissed her. The kiss started out as an almost chaste peck and immediately grew into something hot. Just about the time she was going to open the door and pull him in for privacy, he let go of her. His white teeth gleamed in a grin.

"I have a present for you, sweetheart," he announced, hoisting up the bundle.

"Another one? Taye, you shouldn't have." The words were automatic, the product of a childhood with a mother who drilled good manners into all four of her sons and her only daughter. "What is it?"

"Come with me," he invited. "This isn't just from me. It's from the whole Pack."

Every member of the Pack must have been in the rec room, smiling at her like eager children. Taye led her through them and out to the yard and around the back to where the stable was. The entire Pack followed along behind her. There was a mare there, a solid bay with a white blaze that ran over her nose to a point between her eyes and white stockings on both front legs.

"This is Wind in the Grass," Taye murmured. "She's got endurance and speed enough to carry you away from danger. She is yours. A gift from the Pack. Go, make her acquaintance."

Carla wanted to run to the horse, but she controlled herself and approached gently. By the looks of her neck and head she had some Arabian in her, but her body was strong and blocky, her legs sturdy. The mare seemed calm, and let Carla look in her mouth, but watched everything carefully. Carla guessed she was three or four years old.

The man with the sweet smile, Quill, came out of the stable with a saddle and a pad. "This saddle is for you, Lupa," he said through his hair. Carla's hand itched to pull that mass of golden brown curls back so she could see his face. "It will be in the tack room when you're ready to ride."

Taye caught her sleeve. "Not tonight, sweetheart." He bent to murmur in her ear, "If you want to ride tonight, I'm at your service."

It took Carla a second to catch his innuendo. She blushed and gave him a wild look before noticing the members of the Pack were smiling wickedly. She blushed harder and gave Taye a glare. Taye smiled angelically.

Taye and the Pack took her back to the rec room to the table near the fireplace and swept an arm at a chair set beside the fireplace. Carla hadn't seen that chair before. It was deeply padded and upholstered in leather.

"This is your chair," Taye told her. "Mikey and Alec made it for you."

Two men stepped forward, both with Native American features, but with their dark hair cut short like Taye's They were shy, but clearly proud of their creation as they showed off how the padded arms could be lowered so they wouldn't be in the way while she played her guitar. Carla was touched and thanked them sincerely for the gift. Then Taye unwrapped the big bundle he had been carrying earlier.

"Here are a few things for you until we can go shopping for new clothes for you." First he held up a pair of loose pants with a drawstring waist, then a dark blue button-up shirt. Then, like a magician pulling a rabbit out of his hat he unfolded and held up a full-length leather coat lined with dark fur. "I promised I would dress you in fur like a Russian princess."

The wolves all howled when Taye helped her put it on. It was double-breasted, fastening with buttons

159

carved from bone. The hem hit her just below the knee. Taye put his arms around her from behind and breathed deeply against her neck. "When I'm not near to keep you warm, this will," he murmured into her ear.

The light brush of his lips made her shiver. "It's beautiful."

"You are beautiful," he corrected.

Though they had spoken softly, the Pack heard and howled agreement. "You're our Lupa!" said one man. "Only the best for our Lupa!" shouted another. "Kiss!" called Sky.

Taye grinned at the teen and tilted Carla's chin to kiss her tenderly. Carla's stomach growled, and Taye stopped grinning at Sky's disappointment at the tame kiss to frown down at Carla. "You're hungry."

"She didn't come out for lunch, Chief," said Sky.

"You missed lunch *again*?" Taye asked, exasperated. "How will I ever get you to fatten up if you don't eat? Pack, this is an order: if I am out and your Lupa doesn't come for a meal, pick her up and carry her to the dining hall. Understood?" The wolves all agreed loudly. Carla thought they were teasing her, but their faces were serious. "Come on, sweetheart. Let's get supper."

Carla took the coat off and laid it over her new chair. She let her fingers stroke over the fur when she looked at the Pack. "Thank you, everybody. I've gotten some really nice presents in my life, but none as special as these. Tonight I'll play all the songs I'm going to play tomorrow at the library as a thank you for you."

The wolves howled again, grinning at her. Supper was roasted venison. Carla's chunk was actually well-enough cooked that she didn't need to take it back to finish cooking it. Taye spend the entire meal focused on her. There were long hot looks and times when he bent near to take deep breaths of her scent at her throat, but he also told her what he usually did with his days. He hunted for meat both as a man and wolf, and spent a lot of time training the younger wolves in hunting and fighting. Such hunts and training sometimes took him away from the den for weeks. It would be a while before he would leave his new mate for such a long time (he leaned close to inhale her scent at her nape when he said that, making her shiver), but soon he would begin being away for a night or two a week so they could stock up on meat for the winter. He traveled into town and to smaller settlements nearby to arrange trades for the hides and dried meat from the hunting to obtain the items the Pack couldn't produce themselves like sugar and flour and cloth. As the Alpha, he sometimes judged disputes for the Pack and the humans under the their protection, and he often went out to visit the Clan on the plains. As Lupa, she would be expected to settle any issues while he was away. She was uncertain about that.

"What kind of disputes?" she wanted to know.

Taye sopped up the juice from his meat with bread and popped it in his mouth. He chewed, thinking. "Different things. Last week Denny Preston came to me because his neighbor's sheep kept getting out of their pen and eating his garden." Taye shrugged. "I told the neighbor to build a taller fence and if it happened again he would have to give one of his sheep to Denny. A lot of the time it's a man asking for an extra share of meat. That's pretty typical. Last summer Bob Rakowski asked for help escorting his daughter Daria to her wedding at the Old Fort settlement. I sent a dozen of the Pack along, half in wolf shape and half in human shape." Taye laughed in remembering. "It's a good thing Bob asked for our help. While they were fording the river some woman stealers ambushed them. If it would have been just Bob and his sons, the girl would have been taken. But the ambushers didn't expect wolves."

The wolves, even the ones furthest away, heard every word and began boasting about which of them had killed which ambushers. Taye saw the horrified look on Carla's face.

"What's wrong, sweetheart?"

"You *killed* those men?"

Taye raised a cool eyebrow. "Men who were trying to steal a woman under our protection and kill her escort? Of course. What else would we do?"

"Arrest them! Put them in jail for a trial."

Taye was familiar with the concept from reading books from the Times Before. "We don't have a jail here and no trials, especially for something like this. I am Alpha and you are Lupa; we are the judges over our people and those who would hurt them." He feathered callused fingers over her temple. "Don't worry, sweetheart, it doesn't happen often. Let's talk about something else. Aside from singing for strange men, what would you like to do?"

Carla told him that she was willing to take charge of the kitchen, as long as she had helpers to do some of the work. She would knit socks and sweaters to help keep herself warm in the winter. Other than that, she would care for her horse and ride, write music and play her guitar, and hopefully, make friends and visit them. Yes, she agreed when Taye voiced concerns over her safety, she would take an escort of wolves whenever she left the den. She couldn't imagine anyone stupid enough to try to bother her. But those men the night that Taye first brought her home had been stupid enough to try.

Taye leaned so close they were almost glued together from knee to hip to shoulder. "And someday

163

you'll have children to take care of," he murmured in her ear.

Yes, after her contraceptive wore off. Carla wondered what sort of children they would have. Would the boys be wolves? Would they have a little girl? Carla would like a little girl. Of course, she would have to be careful that her daughter wouldn't turn into a brat. Taye would spoil her rotten, and so would the rest of the Pack. And good luck finding a boy to date that Taye would approve of. She pitied any boy who tried to lure their daughter into the back of his pickup—or whatever the equivalent would be here.

Her future didn't seem terribly exciting. Except, she amended when Taye's eyes smiled into hers while his fingers crept up the inner seam of her jeans, for the nights. Taye's lovemaking was plenty exciting, and teaching him that she intended to be a full partner and not a doll for him to tease would be fun too. And if this concert at the library went well, maybe she could convince Taye to let her do other shows either in town or in the nearby settlements.

Her concert for the wolves that night was a hit. For feral murdering wolves they were amazingly tenderhearted. They cried at her love songs and laughed at the children's songs, and cheered when she sang about soldier coming home from the desert. When she spoke a little about Mr. Gray and his wife's guitar that he had given to her, they all nodded seriously, and then sobbed out loud when she sang about sweet Kylie and the guitar her husband treasured. Taye had tears in his eyes when he leaned close and kissed her gently at the end of the song.

"That was wonderful, sweetheart. You made that up yourself, didn't you? You are—" Kiss. "—so—" Nibble at her ear. "—talented." Another kiss that parted her lips for his tongue to glide against hers. "Let's go to bed."

Carla flashed a smile at him, already planning to take control this time. But as she was putting her guitar in the case three men came into the rec room. Carla recognized Jay and Des but not the third man, who was dressed like an extra in the movie *Dancing With Wolves*, with a breechcloth and hair in two braids past his waist. Carla did a double-take, not because his clothing was odd, but because he was wearing clothing at all. Jay and Des were naked. Taye nodded at them, suddenly alert and passion forgotten. "Report."

Des nodded back, and spoke to Taye, but his words were for all the wolves. "Chief, good news. Your cousin, Wolf Shadow, has found his mate. She is brave and beautiful. She was walking alone on the prairie trying to find help for the ones injured in the airplane—"

165

He spoke the word slowly like it was foreign. "—crash when he found her. There are twenty-nine unmated women from the Times Before and three girl children, but most of them are injured. The Grandmother sent us back to ask for supplies to care for the women."

Carla felt her stomach drop. "Only twenty-nine? And three kids?" she cried. "But there were more than that on the plane. What about the men?"

Des shrugged unconcernedly. "A lot of them died."

"But at least six of the men weren't hurt that badly! What about them?"

Des shrugged again, and Jay said matter-of-factly, "The Clan doesn't have enough food or medicine for everyone. Saving the women is more important than helping a few men who will only try to take the women for themselves."

Taye's arm restrained her from jumping forward. "You killed them?" she shrieked.

"No, Lupa. They died on their own, except for the two we eased. Their infections would have killed them eventually, and with a lot of pain. We spared them that."

"But what about antibi…" Carla was appalled. "No antibiotics?"

"Sweetheart, medicine is hard to get here. We wouldn't murder helpless men, but neither would we

166

allow them to suffer. If your horse had a badly broken leg and there was nothing you could do to save her, wouldn't you give her merciful end?" Taye tightened his arm around Carla's shoulders to comfort her and looked at Des. "Did you or any of our Pack that went with you find their mates?"

Des tightened his face, as if to force back any sorrow or anger. "Wolf Shadow and a few others from the Clan found mates." He glanced quickly at the stranger with him.

"Which women?" Carla asked. She didn't know any of those women well, but after working together with them to save others she felt a special bond. Besides, they were all that was left of her old world. "Taye's cousin's wi—mate. Who is she?"

Jay answered in a dreamy voice. "Her name is Glory, and she is glorious. So soft and round." His hands moved as if stroking generous curves. "And her hair is *pink*. I didn't know hair could be pink."

Carla remembered her, a free-spirit Goth type with surprisingly down-to-earth manners in a crisis. Taye looked at her questioningly. "Do you know her, sweetheart?"

"I know who she is. She was one of the ones who volunteered to walk to try to find help, but I never saw her before we were on the plane."

The wolves were on their feet, almost trembling with excitement and hope. Taye nodded at them. "Sky, Black Wolf, Radden, and Snake, get blankets, cloth for bandages, and food together and ride out to the Clan. We will send everyone to the Clan so you can look for your mates, but in groups of four to six at a time. We can't leave the den and the Lupa without protection."

The stranger was looking at Carla with interest. "This is your mate?"

Taye squeezed her shoulders with his arm. "Yes, this is Carla," he said proudly. "Sweetheart, this is my cousin Jumping Stag from the Clan. We call him Stag."

Carla nodded at the stranger, and was surprised by his eyes. They were vibrant blue in his sun-browned face, even brighter than Sky's eyes. He smiled, and Carla saw the family resemblance. His teeth were glowingly white, and the same dimple that Taye hid beside his mouth flashed briefly. She thought he might be about the same age as Taye. "Nice to meet you."

"You were on the airplane too?" Stag asked. "You're from the Times Before?"

Carla agreed that she was.

"I came because your advice is needed. And Taye's. You are happy with him. I can smell it. You care for him. You share your body with him."

"Um, yes," Carla said, embarrassed. But with these

168

wolves and their noses she couldn't lie.

"My mate is from your world. Her name is Sherry. She is beautiful, with skin like that coffee the traders bring, but so skinny and her legs were broken..." He trailed off and took a deep breath. "She says I'm unnatural. A monster. She calls me a liar. No one can make her happy. Please tell me what I can do to make her love me."

Carla sank into her new chair. "You're a wolf, right? Wolf-born, I mean. Has she seen you change?"

"Yes." Stag dropped to his haunches in front of her. Taye settled onto the arm of her chair and put his arm around her shoulders. "We've all told the woman that I will be a good husband. I can provide for her and our pups."

"Well, back in the Times Before we didn't have wolves, only movies—stories about men who turn into wolves and eat people. Horror movies." Carla was aware of the whole Pack listening. "She's probably scared. You have to think of it from her side. The plane she was riding in crashed. That is pretty scary right there. Now she has a stranger—who turns into a wolf—telling her she belongs to him. Can you understand why'd she be scared?"

Stag sighed and looked at Taye. "How did you get your mate to accept you so quickly?"

169

Taye caressed Carla's shoulder. "I was lucky. It took my parents three years, remember? But I promised Carla that I wouldn't demand sex until she was sure she wanted it." He looked down at Carla with an inquiring look on his face. "What did I do, sweetheart, to convince you?"

"Well … You did so many nice things for me. The hot water, and the stove, and the guitar…" Carla had been thinking about this for a while and struggled to put her feelings into words. "You showed me you cared. And I knew I could never go back to the Times Before. I had to make a new life here. You made me feel safe. I didn't even know that until Pete challenged you. I was scared to death of you at first, and I was afraid you would rape me, but you didn't. Pete would have. And you treated me like an equal. Mostly. I felt like you respected me." She fiddled with the end of her braid, frowning. "You made me believe I was important to you."

Taye lifted her hand to press a kiss to her palm. "You are important to me. At first it was because my wolf had chosen you to be my mate. I would have felt like that whoever my mate was. It was natural to want to protect you and make sure you were comfortable. I began to admire you when you took the man who tried to steal you down with a kick. I liked that you could take care of yourself. Liking and admiration and respect are a good beginning for a couple starting a life together. But now it's more than just liking. I love how generous you are to people. You share your music with joy, like you have with the Pack and you will with Mr. Gray and his family tomorrow. And you listen to me when I talk about things that are important to me like my parents, and my new cousin. I love the way you decide what is right and do it, even when I might not like it, like when you insisted on accepting the guitar as a gift. I love you because you make me happy to see you." He kissed her temple tenderly.

Carla forced her tears back. Taye loved her. It was more than just lust for him. She put her hand over the arm he had over her shoulders and squeezed gently. "We were lucky," she told Stag, who was watching them wistfully. "I think it will take more time for you. Be patient with Sherry. Maybe treat her like a sister for a while until she gets used to you. And," Carla paused to clear her throat. "It might be good to wear clothes around her. In the Times Before people didn't run around without clothes on. It makes us uncomfortable."

Stag glanced around the room full of naked men.

"I'm getting used to it now. But at first ... It was pretty hard."

"The Grandmother requires clothing in camp." He

looked at Taye. "Will you and your mate come so the women from the Times Before can see that they can be happy with a wolf?"

Taye nodded. "In a few weeks, maybe. Aren't Shadow and Glory happy together?"

"They seemed to be, the first day. Then Glory found out she couldn't go home, and she went crazy. Poor Shadow is begging her to love him again, but she only punches him and tells him to drop dead."

Taye coughed to cover a laugh. His cousin was fifty pounds heavier than he, and five inches taller, and so fierce that his reputation was known for hundreds of miles in all directions. The mental image of a woman with pink hair defying his ferocious cousin was amusing. "Have you eaten? There's food in the kitchen. Take what you need."

Stag got up and left. Taye bent to kiss Carla on her temple. "Will it be so hard for these women to accept their mates? Lisa seemed happy with Eddie Madison, and you and I care for each other."

"Yeah, but I think that's unusual. And something about the way Mr. Gray spoke makes me wonder how happy Lisa really is. And, you know, I bet most of the women are going to be scared to death at first. Some of those women are probably new widows if their husbands died in the crash. I don't know how it's going to work out."

"Well, let's not worry about it tonight." His lips brushed over the corner of her jaw. "There are several steps we skipped last night—"

Carla stood up and turned to poke her finger into his chest. "No, tonight *I* get to torture *you*."

"No," he smiled. "That's tomorrow night. Tonight I get to continue what I started."

They argued all the way back to their room, and Carla waited until he had closed the door to hold up her hand to make him keep his distance.

"Taye, do you remember that first night when you said you wanted us to always tell each other the truth?"

"Yes," he said warily.

"Well, I know you're the Alpha, and you need to be in charge. And don't get me wrong. I love what you do to me in bed. But it's really important to me to be your partner. Okay?"

"Carla," Taye interrupted. "Did I torture you last night? Truly?"

Carla shook her head. "Not truly. But I want to be able to touch you too. You belong to me just as much as I belong to you."

Taye remembered the promise he made to his wolf last night. "We can take turns being in charge."

"Does someone always have to be in charge? Can't

we just—er—play?"

"I don't know." Taye was honestly troubled. Even as a teenager before his father had died he had automatically taken charge of things. "I'll try. You take charge tonight." To lighten his own tension he smiled. "Be gentle with me, sweetheart."

Carla tugged his face down for a gentle kiss. "It's the least I can do," she teased, "considering how gentle you've always been with me."

She had thought about undressing him slowly, but he was already naked. So she stroked her fingers over his shoulders to his chest and down his flat belly to his already erect penis. It was hard and thick in her hand. Apparently Taye didn't require foreplay to be fully ready to make love. Carla smiled at him. Last night she hadn't really gotten a good look at his body. Now she took her time to explore him, those taut chest and belly muscles, those strong thighs, and finally, that thick maleness. Taye stood still except for a barely noticeable tremor that went through him when she went to her knees and caressed his penis with her lips and teeth and tongue.

"Sweetheart!" he gasped.

"My turn," she growled, almost like a wolf. "Remember what they say about payback?"

She had barely begun teasing him when he lost his stillness. He pulled her mouth away from him and jerked her to her feet.

"If you don't want these clothes ruined you should take them off right now."

His growl was much better than hers. It sent a shudder of delight right through her. She took her clothes off and left them where they fell. Taye was staring at her like she was a steak and he hadn't just eaten a huge meal. Carla knew her body wasn't perfect. Her legs were long and slender, but her breasts were small, her hips narrow, and she had collected a layer of fat around her middle. Taye's expression was a feral mix of hunger and reverence. He picked her up and carried her to the bed. He dropped her onto her back and climbed over her, trying to nudge her knees open with his own. She smiled tauntingly at him and resisted. Perhaps a foolish thing to do when her lover was an alpha wolf used to getting his way. When he ordered her to open her legs wide, she surrendered and let him enter her in a slow, steady drive that dragged a guttural sigh from her. He moved gently inside her with half-closed eyes. The gentleness dissolved into almost violent urgency. The fingers of the hand not supporting his weight moved over her clit, and in only a few seconds, she came in a rush of heat that forced a keening moan from her. Taye followed a second later. The whole thing, from the time Taye had closed the door had taken only a few minutes. She had to admit she didn't really mind, since she'd gotten what she really wanted. Taye made a big thing about making sure she orgasmed before he did, which suited her just fine. Still, she wanted to torture him for an hour next time.

"That was too quick," he announced raggedly, lying beside her getting his breath back, "Next time I am in charge, and that is final!" Then he sighed. "I didn't let you be in charge. I tried but…"

Carla hid her smile against his shoulder. "It was a good try. We'll keep practicing until you get the hang it."

The lamps were almost out, but he let her see his teeth. "Practice makes perfect?"

Carla tickled him, and he retaliated by pinning her wrists to the bed above her head and kissing her. And it started again, but this time it was slow and tender, and he let her caress him almost as much as he caressed her. Afterwards he held her and whispered, "Was that better, sweetheart?"

"Better," she agreed, stroking his chest. "I think we need to practice every night, don't you?"

"Maybe occasionally during the day, too." He let his lips brush over her ear. "I love you, sweetheart."

"Taye," she said seriously. "I couldn't have found a man to love more than I love you even if I'd stayed in

176

2014."

He kissed her hair tenderly.

His heart pounded under her ear, a steady beat, like the soft rhythm of a love song. That sound was, Carla decided as she snuggled against him, the very best sound to fall asleep to.

CHAPTER NINE

This was concert day. Carla spent most of the morning with her new horse, grooming her and letting her get used to being handled by her new owner. Wind in the Grass was a good horse, but had a bad habit of head-butting the groomer. Carla would work on that. Taye came for her in the late morning, telling her she should eat lunch and change now, so they could leave for town. Carla put on the new clothes Taye had given her. They weren't stylish by early 21st-century fashion standards, but they were comfortable, and best of all, they didn't have bloodstains on them. She wore her short, fringed jacket because her new coat would be too warm for the Indian summer day. Two dozen wolves were in the rec room, each wearing a shirt and pants, and even shoes. Taye arranged the men in a military-like formation with her in the center carrying her guitar case. She also saw a few of the Pack in wolf form on guard in front and behind them. Obviously Taye was taking no chances with her safety. It made her smile even as she rolled her eyes at his over-protectiveness.

The last time she had passed through these streets she had been almost numb from exhaustion and fear. Now she looked around with interest, although there wasn't much to see with tall wolves surrounding her. For the first few blocks people came out of their houses to stare at the wolf parade. The next mile was pretty desolate, just empty buildings crumbling into jumbles of concrete. But the last mile or so showed a well-maintained town. Carla wondered how it had looked fifty years before. Probably like other small towns in rural America. A couple of schools, a few small parks, some small businesses with a couple of chain fast-food places, maybe a population of 25,000. Carla could see that the buildings and roads here had been taken care of. People peeked out of their houses at them while they passed, and Carla could hear some low growls when some young men came too close.

"Hey, guys." Carla's voice was not loud, since she knew the wolves could hear her fine. "I want this to be a

179

fun day, okay? We don't want any trouble. No fighting, right? No growling, no biting." She almost added no peeing on the furniture, but kept that to herself. "Just behave yourselves."

Jay was walking close to her, and he didn't bother to keep his voice down. In fact, he seemed to speak to the dozen men watching them pass. "As long as no one gets too close to you we won't have to kill anybody."

Carla almost growled herself. "Honestly!"

Taye dropped back from his position at point to walk with her. "We'll do only what is necessary to keep you safe," he promised.

Carla didn't think their ideas of what was necessary for her safety quite matched her own. She resolved to be very careful about getting too close to anyone today.

The library was a stately stone building constructed, according to the cornerstone, in 1962. Carla waited outside in a circle of wolves while a few men went inside to check for any traps. "Overkill," Carla muttered to Taye.

He raised a cool eyebrow. "If you want to be able to go places and play your music for strangers, you better get used to overkill."

She almost tripped. "Really? You'll let me?"

Taye kept his face cool and watchful of their surroundings, but tenderness hummed in his voice.

"How can I deny you something that gives you so much happiness? But no arguments about security will be allowed."

She smiled like the sun. "Got it. No arguments."

There was a small entryway and then a large open area with a skylight. The floor was bare polished granite tiles in contrasting colors laid out in geometric designs. At the center of one design stood Mr. Gray and a woman with short, graying brown hair and a tight smile. Wooden chairs were lined up in rows behind him, and six-foot-tall bookcases stood in neat rows on the other side. Carla's escort peeled away to stand in groups of two or three along the wall by the door to let Taye greet Mr. Gray, and maybe that was what made the woman's smile relax. Even fully dressed the wolves looked feral and dangerous. Carla hadn't thought of them as dangerous for some time now. After watching them sob over a sad love song it was hard to see them as scary.

"Mrs. Wolfe," Mr. Gray said warmly. "I'm so glad you were able to come. Thank you for bringing her, Taye."

Taye nodded formally, almost a bow. "I am in your debt. It gives me joy seeing Carla light up when she plays her new guitar." He looked sideways at the woman with Mr. Gray, too polite to look directly at her.

"This is my daughter-in-law, Annie Drummond Gray. Doug's mother."

Carla thought the woman was way too young to have a son in his twenties. "Nice to meet you."

Mrs. Gray turned her head to the bookcases lining the nearby wall. She crooked her finger. "Come out, Ellie, and meet your cousin."

Carla felt Taye stiffen beside her, like a bird dog fixed on a pheasant in the grass. A small, slender teenager with smooth, glossy mahogany hair flowing down to her waist and a plain gray-blue dress that covered almost all of her quietly stepped out from between two bookcases. Her brown eyes were large and a little frightened, moving from the wolves by the wall, to Taye, to Carla, and back to Taye. Mr. Gray put a hand on her shoulder.

"Ellie, this is your cousin Taye Wolfe and his wife, Carla Wolfe."

Ellie bobbed a curtsy. Carla had never seen anyone curtsy before. But then poor Ellie had grown up in that weird farming community where women were second-class citizens. They probably had a lot of weird habits. Carla waited, but Taye didn't speak. So she did.

"We're very glad to meet you, Ellie. Taye has been looking forward to it."

The girl's big brown eyes peeked up at Taye. Carla realized she was only five feet tall. Taye was more than a foot taller. "I am pleased to meet you, too. I've always wanted to know my cousin Taye."

Taye leaned forward and inhaled. "You smell a little like my mother."

Ellie swallowed nervously. Carla wanted to hit Taye and tell him to cut that out. The girl didn't know what he was doing, and she was looking kind of scared now.

"That's a compliment," she told the girl hastily. "Wolves have a really good sense of smell. Don't be— uh—" Freaked out? "—worried. Taye would never hurt you."

"Never," he agreed emphatically. "We're family."

Ellie smiled brilliantly at him. "I'm so glad. Can I hug you? Or do wolves not hug?"

Taye pounced on her, and she was so small she practically disappeared in his careful embrace. "Wolves hug, cousin."

Ellie's thin arms held him tight for a moment. As soon as she let go, Taye gave one more pat on her back and stepped back. "May I call you Cousin Taye? Cousin Taye, I am so glad to know you. I wish I could have known you sooner. My father..." She hesitated. "I'm sorry that..." Her hands fluttered helplessly. "I'm sorry."

"You aren't your father, cousin."

Ellie smiled more comfortably and turned to Carla. "I'm glad to know you too, Cousin Carla. Have you been married to my cousin long?"

Carla thought and was shocked by how short a time she had known Taye. "No, only a few days actually. He won me in a Bride Fight."

Ellie's wide eyes got wider. "Oooh, how romantic!"

That was not the word Carla would have used. "How old are you, Ellie?"

"I've turned seventeen."

She looked even younger, Carla thought, and as delicate as a porcelain doll. "And you're getting married soon?"

"Not until next summer. Grandpa Gray says a woman shouldn't get married until she's at least eighteen." She flipped a pert smile over her shoulder at Mr. Gray. "I'd be glad to marry Neal right now though."

"So you want to marry Neal Overdahl?" asked Taye quickly.

"Oh, yes! He's so handsome and sweet, and not too old. I hope you don't mind we invited him to come today."

"No," said Taye a little grimly. "I'd like to have a few words with him."

Carla felt a spurt of pity for the young man.

Mr. Gray's wrinkled face creased with poorly hidden amusement. "Mrs. Wolfe, Lisa and Eddie Madison are in my office. Maybe you'd like to see her before you start singing? Most of the guests won't arrive for another hour."

Taye saw the excitement in Carla's face. "You would like to see your friend, wouldn't you, sweetheart. I'll take you."

Ellie looked disappointed but smoothed her face immediately. Carla patted Taye's arm. "That's okay. You should stay here and spend more time with Ellie. I'm pretty sure I'm not going to be kidnapped in a library."

Ellie perked up and Taye hesitated. Mr. Gray stepped in. "Taye, I know Ellie will be safe with you. Perhaps you would take her to the refreshments table and chat with her while she gets the cookies and cider ready. Some of your Pack could escort Mrs. Wolfe to my office."

Taye nodded and flicked his fingers at Jay. Jay and two other men detached themselves from the wall. Carla muttered, "Overkill," under her breath, but Taye's expression reminded her she had promised to not argue over security, so she let the wolves surround her. One was Quill, and he was staring at Ellie with his green eyes for once unhidden by his hair. His sweet smile was nowhere to be seen now. Was he angry at

Ellie? Why? But in a second Quill shook his hair over his eyes and turned his back on Ellie to join the other wolves taking her down a narrow corridor to a closed door. Jay pulled Carla to a stop and went in first, just in case, Carla assumed, some woman stealers had a death wish and were hiding in there. He froze in the door, and Carla shoved to make him move aside.

Oops. Carla snapped her eyes away from Eddie bending Lisa over one arm to nibble at her collarbone. Jay and the wolves were completely silent, mesmerized by this display of passion. Carla must have made some small noise, though, because with one lithe movement Eddie raised Lisa, thrust her behind him, and spun to face them in a half crouch. Right then he looked as feral as any of the wolves.

Carla cleared her throat. "Sorry to—uh—interrupt."

Eddie stood up and came to her with an outstretched hand and a warm smile. For a split second Carla admired his perfect, masculine beauty before she remembered to step away. All three of her escort were bristling and growling, trying to put her behind them.

"Shut up!" she told them. "Remember what I said about behaving?" She smiled apologetically at Eddie. "Let's just pretend we shook hands, okay?" She had always thought Eddie was a decent guy, even when his dad was her jailor. He had been friendly and respectful, and since he had been fixated on Lisa she had felt safe with him. She tried to look around him. "Lisa?"

The blonde model was wearing a plain cotton dress that would have looked like a feed sack on anyone else. On her the simplicity was elegant. "Carla!" She hurried forward, but Eddie caught her wrist and gave what looked like a gentle tug but all five feet ten inches and one hundred twenty-five pounds of Lisa lifted off the floor and landed neatly behind him. Eddie was glaring at the wolves, who were glaring right back.

"Good lord," Carla muttered. "I thought it was just the wolves who acted like that."

Since they were about the same height, Lisa peered easily over Eddie's shoulder and said clearly, "No, Eddie thinks he's a caveman sometimes."

Eddie's glare deepened to a scowl.

"I know exactly what you mean. Sounds just like Taye if a man gets too close to me."

It took some quick talking from Carla and Lisa both to get the men out of the office. With extreme reluctance they agreed to wait out in the hall. Carla said firmly, "Don't hurt him," at the same moment Lisa told Eddie, "Don't hurt them."

The women looked at each other and laughed. The first time Carla had seen Lisa was when she had boarded the plane. She had been flawless, from the tips of her high-heeled boots to the top of her perfectly styled hair, in jeans and a tailored jacket that cost as much as some people's cars, with expert makeup rendering her delicate face radiant. Today she wore a homemade dress, her blond hair in a ponytail and no makeup, and she still looked beautiful.

"Lisa, you look fantastic. How are you?" She did look fantastic, but there were shadows in her eyes. "You and Eddie doing okay?"

"Thanks. We're doing okay. We've sort of been…" She shrugged. "It's a different world here. I don't always act the way Eddie thinks I should. But we're working it out. I know it sounds crazy, but I love him. I think even if someone could wave a magic wand and take me back to the world we came from I wouldn't go. Not without Eddie." She wrapped her arms around herself. "And Taye? I heard—" Her voice sank. "—he's a werewolf?"

"Not a werewolf." Carla remembered his explanation that first night. "Just a guy who can turn into a wolf when he wants. Talk about crazy, huh? It takes a little getting used to."

"Does he bite you? Are you okay?"

Carla clearly remembered where Taye's teeth had been so gently last night and blushed.

"Ohhh," said Lisa knowingly.

"We're okay," said Carla quickly. "He treated me like a princess from the first. None of my boyfriends ever treated me half as good as Taye does. Except for the growling and the overkill guards. But that's only because he wants me safe. He's bossy. But we're working on that. I love him too. Back home how many marriages last forever? Here, the question is, how many marriages break up?" Carla searched the model's face, looking for signs of contentment but not finding them. " Lisa, are you happy?"

Lisa nodded slowly as she sank down on the narrow couch by the fireplace and made room for Carla. "I think Eddie loves me. He's the jealous type, though. I don't know why. Except that he saw a copy of an old magazine. Did you read it? The article that talked about me fooling around on Brent? Eddie believes it! And he thinks I'm really like that." She clenched her fists in her lap. "It's not like I'm running around town seeing other men. Back home a lot of men said they loved me because I'm rich or I'm famous or even because I'm beautiful. I'm too skinny to be considered beautiful here. Eddie keeps trying to make me eat more. If he only knew what my hips will look like in a few years…!"

Lisa's attempt at humor fell apart, and Carla could see she was fighting tears. "But, Lisa, when I first came in you and Eddie looked pretty happy."

189

"Oh, sure." Lisa carefully wiped her eyes. "The sex is great. And it's not like he yells or hits me or anything like that. He just doesn't trust me. I … I guess I'm used to flirting. I don't even think about it. I just do it. It makes him crazy, though."

"He needs to quit being so insecure and grow up," Carla said bluntly.

Lisa squeezed her hand and began to talk about her mother-in-law's cooking lessons. The women sat facing each other on the couch and talked for over a half hour. Neither had known the other a few weeks ago, and in their old lives they probably wouldn't have been friends. But they had lived through catastrophe together, and there was no one else who could understand where they had come from or what the world they had lived in was like.

"Oh!" said Carla. "I forgot to tell you! The others from the plane have been found. The Clan—that's like an Indian tribe—are taking care of them."

"That's good. I tried to talk Ray into going out, but he wouldn't. I think maybe a couple of Eddie's friends were going to try to find them, but I haven't seen them for a few days so I don't know if they did go or not." Lisa glanced down at her watch, a precious relic of her old life. "Oh, hey! Time for your concert, I think. I can't wait to hear you!"

As soon as they opened the office door the wolves closed in on Carla, and Lisa waited until Eddie put his arm around her waist and stole a quick kiss. "A little preview for later," he whispered. Carla saw Jay's mouth smirk and frowned at him.

There was a stool for Carla at the front of the rows of chairs. Jay stayed right beside her while they walked through the three or four dozen people sitting there. Quill and the other wolf dropped back to take seats in the last row. Quill's eyes were once more fixed on Ellie. Carla waved at Ellie, who was sitting with a skinny young blond man in a sea of wolves beside them, in front of them, and behind them. Taye must have gone into total protective older brother mode. There was one moment of tension when Lisa and Eddie passed another blond man, a little older, but similar in looks to Ellie's companion. Lisa acted like she didn't notice him, but he stared at her with open longing on his face until Eddie said something short and low. Taye watched them carefully until Eddie and Lisa sat down in the front, then he walked to stand behind Carla.

Mr. Gray was sitting in the front row too, with his daughter-in-law and three other women in their thirties and forties. Behind them were Doug, and three girls between the ages of ten and fifteen sandwiched tightly between a whole bunch of men and boys who looked a lot like Mr. Gray. These must be his family.

Carla opened her guitar case and began checking the strings. As she did that she spoke in loud clear tones. "Good afternoon, everyone. I'm Carla Wolfe, and I'm going to be singing and playing this beautiful guitar today for Mr. Gray. This guitar was his wife's, and when my husband Taye decided to give me a guitar, Mr. Gray brought two instruments to us for me to choose from. I chose this one, because it had such a rich sound. This kind of sound—" She strummed a chord, letting the sound die gradually away. "—comes only from an instrument that has known love. Nothing can make that kind of sound except love, and there's not enough money or anything else in the world to buy it. That's why I'm here today. Not to pay for this guitar, but to let Mr. Gray hear it again, and know that love is still strong within it."

She started her show with "Sweet Kylie's Guitar," telling in simple, gentle words about the young girl who was wooed and won by a young Mr. Gray, who took her away from her devastated home on a long journey across Nebraska to a new life in this town. She told about the dark summer evenings along the road when Kylie would play this very guitar and tell her husband how much she loved him in the words of old songs. Carla sang about the guitar carried by Kylie and by Mr. Gray in turns, over the long weary weeks of walking, how they had shared the weight of it between them, and how its rich sound renewed their strength when the road got rough and long.

The wolves, being in public among what might be enemies, were stoic, but Mr. Gray and several of his family were wiping their eyes. Carla moved into one of her lighter songs. No one else except Lisa and Mr. Gray would understand about the lovers playing phone tag and texting each other during meetings, but the melody was bouncy and fun. The folk songs that had been once recorded by Emmy Lou Harris and Gillian Welch were a hit. She sang for almost two hours, pausing only for water and to talk a little to explain some of the songs. All the while she could feel Taye behind her, radiating pride and love. For her last song she got off her stool and addressed the audience.

"Like the first song I sang this afternoon, this one is one I've written since I've come here. It comes from my heart, and it is for my husband Taye."

She broke all the rules by turning her back on her audience to face him. "Taye," she said in a voice so quiet that only the wolves would hear it, "this song says what I feel."

"One bright morning got on a plane,
That's the day the world ended.

193

Feels like I've gone insane,
My world can't be mended.

———

The plane went down in a field,
Of grass and death and dying.
My walk for help my fate sealed,
I was fooled by farmers' lying.

———

I was tricked by farmers' lies,
And sold in town like a slave.
Offered as the victor's prize,
In the Bride Fight that Ray gave.

———

A dozen fought to make me wife,
But I was won by the wolf Taye.
His wolf had chosen me for life
But I said I'd fight him all the way.

———

The wolf chose me,
But I'm not sleeping with the wolf.
The wolf won me,
But I'm not sleeping with the wolf.

SLEEPING WITH THE WOLF

———

But he let me be, let me rest,
Then a challenge was made for me,
And once again Taye was best
And his goodness I began to see.

———

Taye saved me from a cruel fate,
And he treated me so kind
Then I knew he was my mate,
And I found I didn't mind.

———

The wolf chose me,
But I'm not sleeping with the wolf.
The wolf won me,
But I'm not sleeping with the wolf.
The wolf saved me,
Should I be sleeping with the wolf?
If he loves me,
Then I'll love him,
And I'll be sleeping with the wolf.

———

Choosing once, wolves mate for life,

And never ever will he stray.
So I'll love him and be his wife.
In this new world I will stay.

———

The wolf chose me,
The wolf won me,
The wolf saved me
Since he loves me,
And I love him,
We belong to each other forever,
So I'm sleeping with the wolf
Yes, I'm sleeping with my wolf."

She ended the song with a happy smile, and glanced at the applauding audience over her shoulder. Lisa smiled through tears and pumped her fist encouragingly. Taye reached and caught her chin and pulled her face around to his lips. His kiss was very tender.

"Yes," he whispered against her lips. "Your wolf loves you. Forever."

THE END

WOLF'S GLORY

When goth-girl Glory Peterson's plane crashes she walks to find help. What she finds are people living in teepees like it's the Old West. Glory's happy to take a roll in the hay with him while she's waiting for transportation back to civilization, but when she finds out she's gone fifty years into the future and Shadow is a bossy werewolf who thinks he owns her, her attitude changes fast.

Shadow has always hoped to find a mate, and he knows Glory is the woman his wolf wants. If she would just accept him and do what she's told they could be happy together. Shadow is used to giving orders that are obeyed. Glory hasn't obeyed an order since kindergarten, and she's not starting now. When two strong-willed lovers clash, who will win?

Taye and Carla have found their happily Ever After, but what about Taye's cousin Wolf's Shadow and his unhappy pink-haired mate? Their story is told in the second book of the After the Crash series, *Wolf's Glory*.

SEE WHAT REVIEWERS HAVE TO SAY ABOUT *WOLF'S GLORY*:

TOP PICK

★★★★★

"*Wolf's Glory* is so much fun and I loved it! Ms. Barone gives us plenty of detail and a lot of great characters without making it too much… I wish I'd known about Ms. Barone sooner. *Wolf's Glory* is a true delight!"

—*Night Owl Reviews*

TOP PICK

★★★★★

"Ms. Barone's overall series plotline is riveting to say the least … I can't wait to come back to this futuristically challenged old west… Fans of both romance and paranormal alike should absolutely check out this series. Ms. Barone's work is guaranteed to be like nothing else you've ever read.

—*The Romance Reviews*

TURN THE PAGE TO READ AN EXCERPT
FROM WOLF'S GLORY!

CHAPTER ONE

Maybe they were doomed to walk the prairie forever, never finding help. Glory shook her head fiercely. No, that was tiredness and hunger speaking. There had to be people somewhere. This rotted old railroad track would lead them to civilization eventually. Glory threw a desperate look around and saw nothing but tall dry grass and blue sky as far as her eyes could see—just empty prairie as bare as it must have been when the pioneers first settled the West. If she and Jane didn't find help, people would die. Maybe people had already died. It had been over twenty-four hours since they'd left the crash site, and dozens of people had been hurt, some so badly that they hadn't regained consciousness before the rescue teams had left the crash site. Jane still trudged along in her sensible librarian's shoes, but turned her head back to look at Glory, a thin eyebrow raised in inquiry.

"Just hoping I might have missed some sign of civilization," Glory muttered.

She watched Jane pull out her cell phone and try again, for the millionth time, to make a call. Glory sighed when Jane returned her cell phone to her purse. "Still nothing?"

Jane's brown hair, having fallen out of its prim bun, pushed her shoulders when she shook her head. "Maybe a search and rescue team has already found the crash," she said hopefully.

"Maybe." Glory didn't say anything else. What was there to say that they hadn't already said? Their plane had crashed, and the only surviving member of the crew had tried repeatedly to send a Mayday, but the plane's radio didn't work. Nor did any cell phones, and none of the survivors could connect with the Internet to send an email Mayday. The co-pilot had told them that help was certainly on the way, and organized the efforts to free those trapped by the debris and make the injured more comfortable.

"Perhaps the co-pilot has gotten the plane's radio to work by now." Jane persisted in her cheery optimism.

An optimist Glory was not. "Fat chance," she grunted as she stumbled over the rough ground. "She spent hours trying to call, right?"

"Yes. She did." Jane was slightly subdued, but lengthened her stride in determination. "Now it's up to us to find help."

Glory had to hand it to Jane. She had plenty of energy and enthusiasm. And she had to hand it to the co-pilot. Even with her ankle smashed to smithereens, she had kept it together. She had done everything she could to get the passengers help. But hours later, with no help yet on the scene and medical aid desperately needed, she had asked for volunteers to pair up and walk for help. Glory had volunteered, and so had a bunch of others. The co-pilot rejected some as too young or too hurt, leaving six to be paired up into three teams that she sent in different directions. Glory had been paired up with Jane Harris, a forty-something librarian from St. Paul, and they'd been walking since yesterday afternoon without finding any sign of people at all. The prairie seemed eerily empty.

Glory caught up with the librarian and resumed walking. "You know, I was so excited yesterday morning when I got on the plane in Minneapolis," she ranted. "Four years as a glorified aquarium cleaner at the Mall of America's Underwater World, and I finally landed a face-to-face interview with an international ocean-life study center. Dream come true, you know? It's the reason I got my degree in marine biology."

"Yes, you mentioned that," Jane murmured drily. "Repeatedly."

Okay, maybe Glory had already had this conversation a couple dozen times, but … "Dammit!" Glory swore when her low-heeled pump got caught in the thick grass covering the rail, making her stumble again. Damn, that hurt. Jane gave her a prim glance of reproach, and Glory forced back more curses at her new shoes.

"Are you okay?" Jane asked.

Glory wondered what Jane would say if she cut loose with her normal repertoire of four-letter words, and cleared her throat. "Fine," she grumbled. "Why did I buy these stupid shoes, anyway? Oh, yeah, because they go with this stupid business suit."

"You want to make a good impression at the interview," Jane said, looking approvingly at the boring business suit Glory was wearing and less approvingly at her hair.

True. Glory wanted the job so much that she had bought the sedate navy blue trousers and jacket for the interview. She doubted her usual dressy goth gear of black jeans, black satin bustier over a blood-red silk

T-shirt, and ankle-length black duster would have impressed them much. Too bad. She loved the way the bustier cinched in her waist and emphasized the curve of her hips. She was a big woman, but she had all the curves a woman could want. And then some. Her figure was more along the lines of Marilyn Monroe than Tyra Banks. Too bad ultra-thin was in and ultra-curvaceous was out. Her best friend Jill always said Glory would have been a sex goddess in another era.

"Yeah. Like this outfit is going to impress anyone now. It's ruined."

"I'm sure your prospective employer will reschedule your interview. You can wear something else to that one and do something about your hair color. Our misadventures are completely out of our control. It's probable they are already aware of the crash. I'm sure that by now rescue teams have found the crash site."

Geez, talk about Miss Pollyanna. The never-ending wind blew Glory's hair into her eyes, and she shoved it behind her ear with an impatient hand. She had stripped the purple, red, and black streaks from her hair and changed it to a pink that matched the blouse she'd bought to go with the suit. Yesterday before boarding the plane she'd smoothed it into a sleek French twist. Now it blew like a ragged curtain over the tops of her shoulders. She had left her nose ring and the rings for her left eyebrow at home, wearing only a tiny fake-diamond stud in her nostril, with a matching pair of studs for her ears. When she had boarded the plane she had looked like a successful business person. A little boring ... Well, a lot boring, but she really wanted this job. They were supposed to land in San Francisco at 2:36 p.m. Pacific time, and her interview was at 4:00. She figured she'd have time to touch up her hair and makeup in the airport ladies' lounge before taking a taxi straight to the interview.

Well, she had missed the job interview, and her new suit was ruined by her misadventures. She liked that word—misadventures. It sounded better than "her shitty luck."

"You're probably right." Glory tried for some of Jane's optimism. "They'll reschedule the interview, won't they? Sure, they will. After all, we're heroes, braving the wilderness to get help to save the rest of the passengers." The cheerfulness died when she stepped on a rock and bit off another four-letter word. "It never seems this hard in the movies."

"Heroines," Jane corrected. She smiled, but it was sober. "You're right. The movies make things look comfortable and quick. But we're still better off than the ones left at the plane."

So many of the passengers who had boarded the

plane yesterday morning had been killed, including the little girl whose whiney complaints about not being able to run around had made Glory want to slap her during the first hour of the flight. Remembering her made Glory feel sick. What was she doing, worrying about her clothes and her feet and her interview when that little girl would never have a chance to grow up and have a job at all?

Hey, was that—? Glory squinted at a distant low hill. Yes! Something had moved out there! People? Her heart pounded so hard it felt like it was making the stupid ruffles on her fuchsia silk flutter.

"Hey, Jane, look! Look!" She jabbed Jane in the arm to bring her attention to the dots bobbing along in the distance and began hollering and waving her arms madly. Jane was more sedate, but she waved her arms too.

"Thank God," Jane said. "Finally, we've found help."

The dots came closer, turning into a half-dozen people on horseback, with a bunch of big dogs running alongside. Glory gaped as they rode up to them at a gallop and formed a circle around them, the horses kicking up so much dust that she began to cough. What the hell? When the dust settled a bit she could see that they were Indians. They had long black hair and bare brown bodies made barely modest by a strip of fabric that covered their important bits in front and back but left their chests and legs bare. Every last one of them was model handsome. Damn. Their bodies, unconcealed by clothing, were mouthwateringly perfect. What was this, a movie set? These guys looked like they were actors in a *Dances With Wolves* movie. The dogs were *huge*. She thought they were wolves, but they were too big for that. Maybe a mixed breed? One of the dogs came right up to her and sniffed her crotch. She slapped at its muzzle, shouting, "No! Bad dog!"

Some of the Indians looked shocked. Laughter bubbled in her throat. Hysteria? Gloria refused to do hysteria. She swallowed hard to force it back. The dog stared at her for a minute, grinning at her with its tongue hanging over sharp teeth, then trotted off and disappeared behind the horses surrounding her.

She turned her attention back to the Indians, searching them for phones. She didn't see any phones, and none of them wore enough clothing to hide a cell phone in, so she supposed they didn't have any with them.

"Um." Glory had to clear her throat to cut through the dust coating it. "Hi. Sorry to interrupt. But can you help us? Our airplane went down back that ways and … and … Wow."

Another Indian walked between the horses, tightening the string around his waist that held his diaper thing up, and Glory completely forgot what she'd been saying. It *was* a movie set! That was her favorite wrestling star in makeup and a really long black wig. And very little clothing. Yowza. He was living proof that guys like the ones on romance covers really did exist. She swallowed, wiping a hand over her chin in case she was drooling, and started over.

"Hi. Look, sorry to bother you, but our plane crashed, and we need help. Like an ambulance. And…" Her voice trailed off again because all these men were looking at her very strangely and sniffing the air. She and Jane weren't freshly bathed, but, geez, talk about rude. "Hey!" She snapped her fingers. "Listen up! This is important."

Jane gave her a patient look and took over. "Yes, gentlemen, Glory is correct. We need immediate medical assistance. There are approximately three dozen injured at the crash. Our cell phones are not working. They may have been damaged in the crash, or perhaps there's no coverage here?" Her voice lifted at the end, inviting them to make a call for an ambulance.

Glory restrained herself from rolling her eyes. Jane was a nice lady, boring as beige paint, but nice. But who talked like that? Glory had a master's degree in biology, and she didn't talk like a prissy British butler. She and Jane were total opposites. Glory listened to Nine Inch Nails and Linkin Park; Jane loved Bach. Glory and Jane both loved to read, but Glory liked hot vampire romances; Jane read literary masterpieces.

The romance cover model look-alike ignored Jane. He stepped even closer to Glory, and boy, did he smell good. She took a couple quick breaths to savor his scent. What cologne did he wear? Something spicy and so yummy that she wanted to push her nose into his neck and inhale. He growled something over his shoulder without taking his eyes from her. She should try to pay attention to what he was saying, but damn, he was so gorgeous she had trouble focusing. Any movie with a hot piece of eye candy like this guy would get her money at the ticket booth. And if he was dressed like he was now, they'd get her money multiple times. Holy cow, he was so big and buff he made her feel like a size ten.

"Look," she told him. "Mister ... um ... I'm really sorry to interrupt your movie stuff, but like Jane said, people are hurt. We need to get them some help right away."

"You can call me Um if you want," he said in a low rumble that made her want to melt into a puddle of feminine goo at his feet. His smile was quick and white.

"My name is Wolf's Shadow. What is your name?"

Yum, is more like it, she almost blurted. "Gloria Peterson. Well, Glory. And this is Jane Harris." He was really into his part. Unless he wasn't an actor? It sure looked like he must be an actor, or maybe a model, with that handsome face and even more handsome bod. How many guys looked that good, especially wearing only a diaper? Well, not a diaper. A breechcloth. It showed off the side of his body from ankle to armpit very nicely. He must do some serious lifting, to have such a well-developed physique. Glory could look at him all day. Too bad they didn't have time for that. "Can you help us? Do you have a phone?"

He looked from her to Jane, a slight frown pulling his brows toward each other. "We have no phones. Where are your men? Why did they send two women out alone?"

Glory swelled with tired outrage at his critical tone, but Jane's voice was mellow. "All the men are injured or killed. There was no one else to go for help."

Wolf's Shadow turned his head toward another of the Indians, and the wind lifted his hair. Was that shiny black curtain falling down his back and brushing his butt real? Holy crap. "Stag, take the others to the injured." He looked at Jane and indicated one of the other men. "My cousin Jumping Stag has medical

210

training. He and the others will go with you to help your friends. I will take Ms. Peterson back to our camp to rest."

Glory was tired, and her feet in their new pumps were killing her. But Jane must be just as tired. Neither one of them had slept well last night. Without sleeping bags or a tent to keep them warm, they had huddled so closely together that in some cultures they would be considered married. It was one of the few mornings in her entire life that Glory had been glad to see the sun come up.

"Jane is tired too," she began. "I don't think we should separate. The co-pilot said we should stick together."

Wolf's Shadow frowned. "You will come with me to camp," he ordered.

Glory eyed his magnificent physique with disgusted appreciation. Wasn't that just the way it went? Guys that good-looking were just naturally bossy. It came from being used to getting what they wanted. Too bad for him she was used to going against the flow. "Sorry. We're sticking together. No offense or anything, but I don't even know you."

For some reason that made him smile approvingly. "Don't worry. I promise my intentions are strictly honorable."

Pity, thought Glory.

Brandi Spray Photography

ABOUT THE AUTHOR

Hello, I'm Maddy Barone. I have a B.A. in History, which is probably why I work in the financial department at Medicare. I am a baroness in the Society For Creative Anachronism, an international educational organization which studies the Middle Ages and Renaissance, where I get to dress up in clothes from the Italian Renaissance that I sew myself. In my free time (which is shrinking rapidly since I began writing) my three rescue cats and I enjoy spinning and knitting. Well, they enjoy trying to unwind every ball of yarn they can get their paws on and seem to think that I am playing a game by trying to hide it. Sigh.

I love to hear from readers. Come visit me at *www.maddybarone.com*.

Made in United States
Troutdale, OR
08/25/2023

12373424R00130